BOUND BY DRAGONS

BOUND BY DRAGONS
BOOK ONE

ALISHA KLAPHEKE

Cover Art by CoverDungeonRabbit

Case Character Art by @allexandracurte and Miblart

Editing by Laura Josephson

 Created with Vellum

To all the ladies who long to fly high and breathe fire

FOREWORD

Bound by Dragons is set in the Shrouded Mountains, an area within the Realm of Lights—the Seelie Fae kingdom first presented in The Fae King's Assassin. This short novel can be read on its own, but if you have read The Fae King's Assassin or The Unseelie King's Rebel, you will enjoy the cameos of places and characters from those books.

Bound by Dragons is the first in a true series which will follow the same couple.

CHAPTER I

TAHLIA

At twenty-one, Tahlia still had plenty of time to change her fate. She would do anything, sacrifice all, work until her fingers bled to make it happen. Even though she was a half-breed and didn't have the right blood or the proper ancestors, she was determined to become a Mist Knight and ride dragons into battle.

Rubbing her cold hands together, she smiled and imagined the feel of the high-altitude wind on her face, the way it would clean the filth from her cheeks. She'd heard people say rank and money weren't the keys to happiness, but those folks had never had to go without food for days on end or been trapped inside the house with the pigs all winter long.

Somehow, she would fly her way out of the life of a lowly squire who picked up after others and away from the poverty she'd lived in since she was a child.

Failure was not an option.

Her friend Fara held their lady knight's mare, Daffodil, by the reins. She raised a dark eyebrow and set one purple hand on a hip.

"Tahlia, I don't like that look. That's the look that says you're about to drag me into trouble."

A cold breeze blew through the snow-laced pines and pulled a strand of Fara's hair from behind her dramatically pointed ear. Fara was a full Fae—unlike Tahlia, who was half-human and half-Fae.

The horse stomped the ground, nostrils flaring, as if she could sense Fara's disapproval. Tahlia brushed the mount's right flank, removing the dried mud the mare had picked up during the journey through the mucky pass into the lower reaches of the Shrouded Mountains.

"Oh, you love trouble. Don't try to deny it." Frustration itched under Tahlia's skin. She longed to move this fate of hers forward more quickly. But so far, no opportunities had shown themselves.

"I like fun trouble," Fara said, "and Tahlia-style schemes are less joyful and more *we nearly died.*"

"Well, you have time to prep yourself because I don't have the plan quite figured out yet."

She snorted. "That has never once stopped you."

Tahlia chuckled as Fara looked down the trail toward the town gate, where their lady had gone an hour ago.

"What's taking her so long?" Fara asked.

Tahlia brushed a cluster of burrs from Daffodil's back leg. "You don't think she could be seeing him, do you?"

Their lady had a former lover in this small mountain town. They'd had an affair when she was much younger, before her father arranged an engagement to a male of his choice. The moment that fellow died from a fever that ravaged their town, their lady informed her father that she would be taking part in the dragon tournament. The lady wanted to become a dragon rider and to be free of her father's machinations. Tahlia didn't blame her one bit, and she only hoped the lady's rise would make her own dream come true that much faster.

Fara glared at the town walls as if she could see through them with enough concentrated effort. Neither she nor Tahlia possessed such magic, so all of this was guesswork.

Fara groaned. "I think maybe so. She's never taken this long at market."

"Did you get a glimpse of that message?" A dove had dropped a note at their camp two days ago.

"No, but her flushed cheeks pointed to some naughty contents. Stones, do you think she's left us for good? I can't handle another day without a meal. I'm not built for this!"

Tahlia blew out a breath. "Eh, it's all right. We will figure this out."

But if their lady decided against heading to the Shrouded Mountains for the event, Tahlia, too, would be stuck in this small dull town for as long as it pleased her ladyship.

Tahlia put the mare's brush in a saddlebag. "I'm going to find out."

"You can't just walk in there and start asking where she is," Fara said.

"Why not?" At the end of the right fork in the road, two guards stood at the city gate.

"Because it could take you hours if not days to find her."

"I doubt that. How hard can it be to locate a female who's six feet tall and dressed in tourney leathers?" This place would be abuzz with the appearance of a lady knight. Not only was she a noble, but she was female and most knights were male.

Fara looked to the sky, her face flushing. "I'm going to kill her if we find her alive."

"I will be back in an hour."

"No, you won't. Not a chance." Fara muttered angrily at the ground, lost in her usual spiral of worrying thoughts.

There was one way to get her friend's head out of the spiral. She had a weakness for gambling. "I bet you half my rations."

Fara lifted her head. "You're on."

Two hours and three inns later, Tahlia had found their lady locked in a chamber with her former lover.

She knocked for the second time. "But, my lady, if you don't go to the tournament, won't your father find out and come after you?" The door at this particularly cheap inn was thin enough to allow sounds of their kissing and more to carry to her ears.

"I don't care!" the lady shouted. "Be gone! You're free to do as you like. I am a lady no longer. I am now the smithy's wife, and I care not for anything my father says."

Pressing her forehead against the door, Tahlia exhaled. This was a problem. A big problem. Without their lady, she and Fara were out of a job. They maybe had one tiny sack of coins between them. Not nearly enough to live on while seeking new employment. Especially since it seemed highly unlikely their lady would be doling out references as to their skills and character.

But the lady would not change her mind. Tahlia knew her well enough to be certain of that sad fact. Running her hands through her tangled black waves, Tahlia left the lady and her lover to their new life path.

Now to figure out hers.

As she maneuvered through the crowded market, Tahlia's past rose up in her mind. She'd lived with her family in a crumbling merchant's home for a few years when her father tried out another of his *grow rich quickly* schemes. That idea had failed like his others. Her father ended up drinking their savings away while Tahlia and her mother worked extra jobs at a nearby pig farm just so they could eat once in a while. She remembered her older brother coming home frustrated from his job, eyes bloodshot and his fists coiled and prepared to hit someone. He never actually raised a hand against Tahlia or their mother, but Tahlia had kept her distance anyway. She knew an animal ready to fight when she saw one. It had been the worst time in her life, spent dodging her brother and suffering the pangs of an empty stomach. Her mother was kind, but Tahlia never connected with her in the way that some did with their mothers. Tahlia had spent the majority of her life thus far hungry and lonely.

But she was finished with that life. As Tahlia made her way toward the gate, dodging a gorgeous family of silver-skinned full Fae with ram horns and a lovely couple with pale skin and tails, she permitted herself to dream big. If you didn't let it all go and just wish hard once in a while, how could you know what might actually be possible?

By the time she reached Fara, she was determined that her time had come.

"Our lady will not be returning."

Fara began stammering, her fangs showing and her lavender lips pulling into a grimace. "Then why are you grinning?"

Tahlia held up a hand. "This is a golden opportunity."

"Please, can't we just head into the town and wait? She might change her mind." But even as she said it, Tahlia shook her head and Fara began nodding, knowing their lady had loved this fellow for years and wouldn't be leaving. "Do you think she had this planned? That the message was from him?"

"It had to be."

Turning the exact shade of a ripe aubergine, Fara handed Tahlia Daffodil's reins and started kicking the bags they had carried on their backs during the journey up to this point. She let loose a string of curses that would have made even Tahlia's horrible brother blush.

"Don't attack our only belongings, Fara. We'll need every bit of bread and dried meat in those bags to survive the rest of the trip to the tournament."

Fara whirled. "What do you mean?"

"I mean that I am going to compete in her place."

"No. We are not going. They'll put you to death."

"Why?"

"Because you're half-Fae. Because your blood isn't gold enough, Tahlia. You know I personally believe that is a stupid measure of ability, but I'm not one of the judges."

"I can use your blood for the testing if they demand a sample."

"And when they catch us, we both die," Fara said.

"If you don't want to risk it, I understand. You can go with my good wishes."

"Well, thanks for that, but you're all I have in the world." Fara's throat moved in a swallow.

Tahlia's chest ached. She took Fara's hands. "You're all I have too, sweet friend, and I want more for us. So much more."

Fara started to pull away, but Tahlia held her friend's fingers and locked eyes with her. Fara's eyes were more slitted than Tahlia's but not by much. Since high Fae skin tones, features, and ears varied so much, no one could tell Tahlia was only half-Fae. But those Fae whose ancestors rode dragons from the beginning of time had a bright gold shimmer to their blood—a byproduct of dragon power seen when a Bloodworker applied certain chemicals. That particular Fae blood was called Mistgold.

"We can do this. I'll be Lady Tahlia of... Lady Tahlia of Northwoods. We can use the isolation of the Mist Knights as a tool. They don't know of far-off small estates. They will believe it if we show confidence."

"You have too much confidence."

Tahlia's grin was untamable. "Maybe, but I can use it to fill our bellies and clothe our backs."

"I don't know..."

"Dragons are just larger horses."

"Ha!" Fara pulled away. "Sure, they're just horses as large as castle stables who breathe fire."

"Who is the best rider you've ever met?"

"You, you arrogant arse."

"Exactly. I was born for this, Fara, even though I have only the slightest hints of Mistgold in my blood. We will be a part of the most glorious culture. The Mist Knights." The name of the group who guarded the Realm of Lights' coastline practically sparkled in her mind's eye. "Once I make my way into the order, you'll have the coin to do exactly as you wish. Stay, leave. Continue to help me or take on a different position. Whatever makes you happy. You can't find that kind of freedom without gold and silver to your name."

"I hate to admit it, but you're right, of course."

"I am, and we can do this."

"Where will you get tourney leathers?"

"I don't know, but I bet you already have an idea."

"They sell sets at the base of the Mist Road," Fara answered begrudgingly.

"Do we have enough to buy one?"

"If our lady doesn't come after that sack." Her gaze flew to the brown bag tied to the horse's saddle.

"She's too *busy* to worry about coming back. To her, that sack is nothing. She has a full purse with her already and a smithy who will make enough to please her." Their lady had never been materialistic like the rest of her family. Tahlia had always respected her for that.

"Fine. But if there is even a hint of the judges being onto you, we leave immediately."

"They won't find out," Tahlia said.

Fara's neck went red, a sure sign of her notorious temper rising. She lifted a finger and shook it under Tahlia's nose. "But if they do..."

Tahlia took her hand and gently lowered her finger. "I was born for this. My blood has gold in it."

"Not enough to pass the Bloodworkers' test."

"Like I said, I can use yours. We're clever. We can get around that. If you're up for it."

Exhaling and breaking away, Fara spun.

She had to agree. Tahlia didn't want to admit it, but she truly wanted Fara at her side. With Fara's support and her blood, this wild plan was actually plausible. Without her, it would be lonely and far more dangerous.

"Please, Fara. Consider it. Let's change our fates. We can do this."

Grasping clusters of her hair and muttering, Fara stared at the sky. "I never should have given you that apple."

Tahlia laughed, remembering the day they'd met when Tahlia had been a slip of a thing—fourteen, half-starved, and desperate. Fara had given up her breakfast so Tahlia could make it to their lady's military event in Seelie King Lysanael's city.

"You know you want to do this with me just a little bit ."

Fara growled and waved a fisted hand at the gathering clouds. "Fine. Let's go before a storm rolls in and makes me even more irritated. But stop smiling."

"You didn't even look at my face."

"I don't need to. I can sense that smile. You're not allowed to have fun doing this. I'm still against it."

"What's life without some risk?"

"Comfortable. And it usually includes cats, which I approve of."

"Dragons beat cats any day."

"Not in my book."

Tahlia chuckled. "Have it your way. No fun on this adventure. Zero. Got it."

But she couldn't help but feel more alive than ever. This was a real chance to grab the life she wanted, to snag her fate from the greedy hands of the Old Ones. A thrill zipped through her blood and she grinned at the sun shining through the breaks in the clouds.

CHAPTER 2
MARIUS

Marius finished tying back his long Fae-white hair as he strode across the foyer of the Mist Knights' castle, a structure that had been carved from the mighty cliffs of the Shrouded Mountains and specifically the peak called Dragon Tail. The pale light of pre-dawn streamed through the stained-glass windows. The click and knock of his boots echoed off the domed ceiling, where powerful crystals half the size of his dragon refracted the windows' glow to scatter complicated patterns over the stone floor. Morning exercises would begin soon.

He pursed his lips and adjusted the whip coiled loosely around his shoulder. The place was empty. Was he the only one awake and prepared for the day's schedule? It wasn't as if he wouldn't rather have a nice lie-in with a hot cup of tea and a novel that he wouldn't want anyone to know he was reading, but now wasn't the time for relaxation.

The ever-present mist of the Shrouded Mountains dampened his cheeks as he left the half-open doors of the foyer and hurried to the tournament grounds. The grounds were devoid of any activity. Frustration lanced through Marius. Could no one follow a schedule?

He threw up his hands and headed out of the tourney grounds and toward the stables just outside the inner gates of the cliffside castle. It was one thing for the knights to sleep in after a festival or during a holiday, but the tournament was days away. There was no time to waste.

The dragon stables were also cut out of the mountain and not even Marius had fully explored all of the inner pathways of the labyrinthine structure that housed the entirety of the Mist Knights' dragon herd.

Outside the large doors, Marius's squire, Remus, was polishing a saddle. The young lad's straw-hued hair hung over his freckled face. He was just nineteen and though he was too jovial for Marius's taste in assistants, he did seem remarkably brave and intelligent.

At Marius's appearance, Remus stood, shoved his hair behind his ears, and bowed. "High Captain, I have your saddle ready. Would you like me to gear up Ragewing?"

Marius wanted to tell the lad to tie back his unruly hair, but he didn't want to be too harsh quite yet. The lad had only started working for him a week ago when Marius's former squire had been promoted to knighthood.

"Thank you, Remus, but you know I prefer doing that myself."

The squire nodded and handed the saddle over. "Ragewing finished his morning meal, sir."

The saddle's smooth seat and straps gleamed in the rising sun's light. The scent of the leather and the smoky odor of the dragons combined to calm Marius and chase away his frustration with the other knights and knights-in-training.

"If I may ask..." Remus swallowed.

Marius grunted. Remus was always asking the most inane questions.

"Why do you need a whip or a bow on the back of a fire-breathing dragon?"

Breathing out through his nose, Marius

attempted to be less surly. It was a challenge he wasn't sure he could conquer.

"Because dragons at their best can blaze maybe five times in a day. When they are injured or battle-fatigued, that capability decreases."

"I would have thought one or two blasts of fire could end any fight."

"Sadly, no. And fire should always be the last resort anyway. It isn't a kind way to kill and should only be used when there is no alternative."

Remus's eyes widened and his lips parted.

"Why do you seem so surprised to hear that?" Marius asked.

"Because you are High Captain Marius Leos Valentius, defender of the Realm of Lights, Shadow of the Shrouded Mountains—"

Marius's cheeks warmed at the praise and he held up a hand. "Please. It's ridiculous to give me all the credit. Every battle was won by a unit of Mist Knights and our dragons. I am only one male and I do nothing without Ragewing and my knights."

"Humble too." Remus whistled quietly and shook his head. "You might hate it, but you're my hero, High Captain."

If the lad knew all Marius had done during those battles, he might feel otherwise. Marius didn't regret his actions, but not all of them felt heroic upon reflection. More like desperation and panic laced with ingrained military skills.

"If that's all, I need to get moving," he said wryly.

The squire bowed. "I'll meet you out here when you are ready, sir."

"Very good."

The entryway to the stables had just enough space for three dragons to pass side by side. Torches blazed along the rough stone walls, lighting the way. Marius walked the familiar path to Ragewing's cave and stopped outside the smaller gate. The cave was dark, lit only by the ventilation holes cut into the ceiling, but the shuffling of a tail along the sweet-scented rushes let Marius know his dragon stood inside.

"Ready to fly, my friend?"

Marius leaned on the waist-high gate and extended a hand. It was never smart to just march into a dragon's cave without first gaining permission from the beast. More sounds issued from the dim enclosure and then a warm snout found his hand. Marius's eyes adjusted to the low light and he gave Ragewing a smile. Ragewing was a Heartsworn, a dragon known for loyalty and intelligence. They were large and fiercely loyal to their riders. Stories had been told of Heartsworns sacrificing themselves for those they loved—other dragons and riders alike.

Ragewing's scales held all the shades of red from scarlet to a color that was nearly pink. His dark orange eyes were slitted like Marius's. The fiery eyes glittered in the low light and the second lid—the one that protected a dragon's sight from fire damage—slipped up then back down again. Ragewing's throat had a golden sheen that swept down his belly and ran along the underside of his spiked tail. He was a gorgeous creature and far larger than the other Heartsworns on the mountain. He was their alpha. Marius sometimes worried about that fact because Commander Gaius's Heartsworn should have been alpha. But dragons were not high Fae and they didn't really respect the Fae ranking system. They had their own way of determining pack leaders.

Running a hand down Ragewing's snout, Marius whispered, "Good morning, my proud monster. How did you sleep? I hope it was a good night for you because we have a host of idiots to deal with this morning. Every last one of them will be late to the grounds."

Ragewing snuffled into Marius's flying leathers and he rubbed the animal's long neck, checking a wound that he'd suffered in yesterday's air sparring with the commander. Dragons healed quickly and the cut appeared nearly mended already. Swinging the gate wide, Marius went inside the cave and began to saddle him. Marius threw the saddle over the dragon's back, then bent to retrieve the rope attached to the girth. Pulling the rope, he found the end of the strap. He untied the rope from the strap and buckled the girth to an appropriate tightness. Ragewing bumped his shoulder and threw a wing over his head.

"Yes, I know. You need a day off. You'll get one very soon. I swear it."

Ragewing truly did deserve a break. He was the hardest working dragon on the mountain, and probably in the world. Normally, they'd be training half days only this time of year, when the pirates had left the coastline due to storms and the commander had no missions for them. But it was a tournament year, so the work just kept coming.

Only one new Mist Knight would be named at the conclusion of the tourney, just one individual who showed the prowess and keen mind of a would-be expert military dragon rider. It was up to the commander to pick the winner from the combatants, but Commander Gaius would ask Marius his opinion.

At twenty-five years of age, Marius was the youngest person ever to be promoted to High Captain of the Fae Mist Knights. He wasn't about to screw up this appointment by failing to rouse those under him to train thoroughly enough. The only one higher in rank than him was the commander, and someday, Marius would take over that position.

It was all part of his plan.

He would marry the commander's daughter, Ophelia—another dragonriding Mist Knight and a great one to boot—and carry on the grand tradition of his people. His blood was nearly all Mistgold, and he and the commander's daughter would produce young that were even stronger. His skill with the dragons was matched only by the commander, but Marius's offspring would be better than either of them.

Your sacrifice won't be for nothing, Bellona.

After his parents had died, his older sister had given up her chance to leave for the healing arts academy and handed over all of the inherited coin to support Marius's training efforts.

Bellona had died shortly after his arrival here.

The courier Marius had paid to deliver his wages to Bellona had informed him that an invading party from the nearby seaside had ripped through the town and killed many. Marius squeezed his eyes shut, recalling the words as they'd spilled from the courier's mouth, those terrible words. *"...horrible tragedy, High Captain..."* Marius pressed a hand to his chest. *"...only a handful of survivors..."*

He still couldn't believe she was gone.

Bellona had valued Mistgold blood and the traditions of their people even more than Marius at that time.

Old Ones bless her wandering soul.

He would make her proud, he thought as he worked Ragewing's bridle into place. If he failed in this, it would be akin to stomping on her grave. No, he refused to be anything less than excellent as he lived out his dream and hers for their family's bloodline. With every pirate he killed on missions, he avenged Bellona's death.

Once Ragewing was saddled and had finished the pear slices Marius had brought for him, the two met Squire Remus and started toward the arena.

"Pears again, hmm?" Remus's lips twitched.

Marius pulled at the gold-embroidered collar of his uniform with one hand and held loosely to

Ragewing's reins with the other. "It's not silly to give a dragon a treat now and then. They trust those who offer fine gifts. It's in their nature."

"Aye, Captain. I'm sure you're right. You probably know more about the beasts than anyone alive."

"The commander knows more."

"All right. Maybe so. But you rode earlier in life, didn't you? He didn't start riding until age thirteen, if the rumors are right," Remus said.

"I rode my first dragon at five."

"Old Ones, but that was young! How did you ever manage that? Who taught you?"

This new squire talked too much. His appreciation of Marius's talent and dedication was nice though.

"My mother and father instructed me at first." Marius didn't care to get into his entire family history right now. "Let's focus on the task at hand, shall we?" He raised an eyebrow at the squire.

The young lad nodded and went quiet.

Three of Marius's fellow knights stood in the arena and a few more were making their way in with their dragons. Ophelia stood ready—he was quite glad his future mate was punctual—while others soared toward the tournament grounds to land beside her and the others.

"Except you three," Marius said, nodding to Titus, Maiwenn, and Morvan, "you are late. You will clean stalls after our morning flight and give your squires an hour off."

"Aye, High Captain," the knights said in chorus.

Ragewing's reins were a soft, familiar texture in Marius's right hand. "Justus, your uniform is wrinkled. Go." He pointed to the castle keep then eyed the rest of the knights. "We can't be less than our best, especially considering the king and queen might arrive soon to watch the tournament. Remember, your tidiness speaks to the attention you show your dragon and your position here. When I see unkempt clothing, I wonder if your tack has been checked properly and if you checked your dragon's scales and their food. Dragons deserve the best care we have to offer."

Justus handed his dragon's reins to his squire, then hurried away to follow Marius's orders.

"First, we will fly in formations. Once I give the signal," Marius said, "Ewan will move out, turn, and fly as our enemy."

"High Captain?" A female Mist Knight named Claudia raised a finger.

"Yes?"

"How many dragons do the pirates have now?"

"At last count, only three. But three very capable full-sized Green-flanked Terrors."

The knights murmured, their wary gazes going to the one Green-flanked Terror in the Mist Knights' herd. Ophelia held that dragon's reins, her blue-green hair rippling behind her. Though she was beautiful, neither his body nor his heart longed for her touch. Only his mind wanted her as his mate because she was a part of his plan. This wasn't about love, but about upholding and protecting the Mist Fae's way of life.

Ophelia glanced at him and her lips shifted into a subtle smile. She never smiled for anyone else. That did please him because perhaps she was indeed willing to go along with his plan.

"Double check your tack now and then we will fly," Marius ordered.

The knights obeyed him, tugging girth straps and running hands over bridles and buckles. Squires prompted the dragons to spread their wings so they could do a last moment look for any injuries or disease.

Justus returned in a properly pressed uniform

and as soon as he seemed ready, Marius climbed into Ragewing's saddle.

"Bow and arrow formation to begin!"

Marius patted Ragewing and they burst into the sky. He would never stop being astounded by a dragon's take-off capabilities.

CHAPTER 3
MARIUS

The dragon expanded his great ruby-hued wings, and then they were flying through the mist and toward the blue sky above.

The rest of the knights followed him into the air and soon the formation was complete. Marius eyed Justus. He kept dropping back too far.

"Stop tugging at her reins, Justus!" Marius shouted over the wind with the power of his Mist-gold blood. Those who had strong blood were usually gifted with the ability to send their voice much farther than other Fae.

The rest of the knights kept nicely in formation, and once they'd flown over jagged Sunthrone—the second-highest peak in the Shrouded Mountains behind the castle's perch—he raised his arm and locked eyes with Ewan. The knight dropped below the formation, wheeled around, then came back at the group blowing third fire, a flame strength only a third of the power his dragon possessed. That level of flame was harsh enough for serious sparring, but not so fierce as to maim anyone if things went wrong.

The formation split into two and sandwiched Ewan and his Spikeback mount. The dragon's pale blue scales and wings made him nearly invisible against the sunlight. Ewan had his dragon drop low and it took Marius a second to notice the shift. Titus and his Spikeback and Atticus on his Heartsworn dove to meet him with mock attacks of third fire.

They missed their target as Ewan, great rider that he was, had his dragon tuck his wings and dive. He knew exactly how to use the color advantages of his mount. Marius and Ragewing shot toward him, then increased speed and looped up under Ewan to drive him back into the tight spot between the formations. Ewan swore as he veered left, taking a flame on his dragon's chest. He steered his dragon away, adopting the movement for a false injury.

"Titus! Morvan! Come around the back of unit one!" Marius tapped Ragewing's shoulder and the dragon whipped himself into formation with unit one.

The two mock enemies flew as ordered then rushed the back of the unit, sending flames in quick bursts.

"Star maneuver!" Marius shot upward, taking the northernmost point of the group's practiced position.

The others darted in all directions, spanning out like stars on a clear night. The mock enemies, Titus and Morvan, went after Ophelia and her Green-flanked Terror, knowing that she was the greatest threat.

Ophelia steered her mount around and let loose a bit more than third fire. Titus's Spikeback wailed and roared. His right wing tip was singed.

"Ophelia! Too much fire. Maintain practice power or you're done for the day!"

And if she showed cruelty to her dragon again, he would punish her as he would anyone else.

She shot him a glare, but the next volley of fire was truly just that and not flames.

Marius glanced at Maiwenn, who rode her Seabreak, a cyan dragon with four wings that could also swim if the need arose. She was his secret attacker in today's practice. Maiwenn gave him a nod and wove her way through unit one, taking out two at a time with the lesser mock fire strikes.

Lifting his arm, Marius made a circle in the air before pointing to unit two, who flew around Morvan and his Heartsworn, surrounding the rider and dragon while they were distracted in their attack on Ophelia.

But none of the riders could catch Maiwenn. Seabreaks were known for speed just as Heartsworns were, but this particular Seabreak had been blessed with a quickness Marius had never seen in a dragon.

Trailing Maiwenn and driving her toward Ophelia, he drew his whip from his shoulder and snapped it toward Maiwenn and her mount's tail. The tip nicked the dragon's last spike, a spot most dragons wouldn't feel unless they were Seabreaks. Maiwenn's mount yowled and turned, eyes flashing with rage.

Leaning over his dragon's neck and winding his whip around his upper arm, Marius aimed his voice at Ragewing's ear. "Wait…"

Maiwenn's dragon opened its maw to breathe fire—maybe to blaze full strength considering how angry she appeared to be.

Marius whispered, "Now."

Ragewing shot upward and the wind blasted Marius's face. He had to hold tightly with both his legs and his arms to keep from falling. He looked over his shoulder to see Maiwenn's flames shooting at Ophelia. He'd turned the two mock allies on one another and they'd been marked enough by lesser flames to show a loss.

Marius led the two units back to the arena.

Maiwenn landed near Marius. "High Captain! That was clever."

"Thank you." Marius hopped off of Ragewing and opened the top of the water trough near the side of the public stands so the dragons could drink.

"I think we should increase our tolerance for fire, High Captain." Ophelia's voice cut the air as she led her Green-flanked Terror to the second trough, where Titus and Ewan were wiping down their dragons and checking for any serious wounds.

"The tournament calls for more aggressive training exercises on the final day. You'll have your moment to show your fire, Ophelia."

He studied her features, trying to get a read on whether or not she was angry or if she had indeed given in to his command. Though he outranked her, it was a delicate situation. Her father was the commander and she had sway due to the familial link even though it was not at all proper. He shouldn't even worry about having to reprimand her, but the commander had shown her favoritism in the past, so he had to watch himself. Marius would have much preferred a unit with clear rank procedures so there was no question as to what actions were permitted. Ophelia's gaze was flat, but she released her dragon's reins and came closer.

She looked him up and down, then almost smiled. "I look forward to the tournament festivities. Will you be accompanying me?"

He inclined his head. "Of course. If you'll have me."

"I *will* have you." Her smile grew teeth and he wasn't sure he liked that tone.

"Good." If she thought she could control him, she was wrong. He would wed her for the sake of Mist Fae blood and tradition, but he would not be cowed by her. They would be equals. Partners. Hopefully, she would be amenable to that situation.

The dragons lapped the water like massive cats, splashing so much that he had to step back to avoid being sullied. Ragewing stopped drinking and eyed him.

"Yes, I know what you are waiting for." He

scooped a handful of water from the trough and poured it over the back of Ragewing's lowered head.

When Marius turned back around, Ophelia was already on the far side of the arena, leading her dragon back to the stables. He needed to tell her how he felt about their future and see what she thought about it. She'd shown interest through body language and finding him at meal times, but was she serious about their impending relationship?

He blinked. He shouldn't think of their potential marriage as impending like one did a sense of doom. No, he didn't feel like that. It was exciting. Correct. A good thing. Yes.

A shudder ran down Marius's back and he froze. What was that?

"You look like you're about to spontaneously combust, High Captain." Remus was standing right beside him, offering a cup of mint water.

"Did you feel that?"

"Feel what, sir?"

A wave of energy had pulsed through the air. Or perhaps he was simply excited for the tournament. "Nothing. Never mind."

"Are you upset about something? You seem pretty distracted."

Marius took the offered cup and drank the cool

beverage down in three swallows. "Thank you. And I'll thank you also to mind your own business."

"You are my business, Sir Marius."

"You know what I mean."

"Do you want me to take Ragewing back?"

The other knights were on their way out of the arena. None of them seemed taken aback by...by whatever that feeling had been. They walked and chatted as if nothing had happened. The next session would take place in the afternoon after the dragons had rested and then flown individually with their riders. All was as normal.

"No, I'll tend him here," Marius said, "and then I'll put him back in the stables myself. You can take an hour off."

"Thank you, sir."

Remus said something else before leaving, but Marius couldn't be bothered to listen. Ragewing lifted his head and eyed the gate leading to the market and the homes beyond the castle keep.

"Is there something on the air right now, Ragewing? I felt odd for a moment." It wasn't as if the dragon could actually answer, but oftentimes, Ragewing found a way to communicate if he was motivated enough.

The dragon bumped Marius's side and snuffed a

hot breath of dragon smoke. The black circles cloaked Marius's view of the arena and gate for a moment. He set to washing the spring pollen from Ragewing's wounded area and tried to let go of both his worries about Ophelia and the strange feeling.

King Lysanael and Queen Revna would arrive soon. He had to remain focused.

CHAPTER 4

TAHLIA

The road leading out of the lower mountains lived up to its name—the Ghost Path. Not only did the mist that always hung heavy in the Shrouded Mountains cover this area, but also the elaborate tombs of fallen Mist Knights walled the snaking line of cobblestones.

Tahlia glared at a tomb topped with stone dragon wings. "These Mist Knights must be a humble sort." She snorted and set a finger on the writing. "Here lies the majestic Julius, master of the clouds and stars. Wonder what one commands the clouds and stars to do? Get you a cup of tea? Or perhaps a back massage?"

Fara laughed. "Check this one out. Here lies

Magnus, bane to pirates and master of the art of love."

"Oh, wow. Can you imagine him requesting that phrase on his stone? Hello, Master Tombcarver. I like to slice and dice bad guys and have seen plenty of action, if you know what I mean," Tahlia said in a stupid, low voice as she elbowed Fara. "Can you word that in your fancy style?"

"I can practically see the Tombcarver's eyes rolling. I'm surprised he doesn't play jokes on these arrogant arsehats."

At the bottom corner of the next tomb, a tiny carved creature caught Tahlia's eyes. "Is that a mule?"

Fara bent to look closer. "It is definitely an ass." Her finger traced the long ears.

"Maybe he did have his own little jokes on these haughty knights and nobles."

Chuckling, Fara jogged to the next tomb while Tahlia held the horse's reins. Purple hair lifting in the wind, Fara knelt at a tomb that had suns carved all over it and pointed at the bottom, in the center. "This one has a rooster crowing so hard its eyeballs are popping out."

Tahlia barked a laugh and Daffodil jumped. Tahlia set a hand on the mare's neck to calm her. "I want to meet this Tombcarver. He seems like our type of Fae."

"I'd buy him a drink if I had any extra coin."

"We are going to have so much gold that you'll be able to buy him the whole tavern."

"Sure, Tahlia. Sure."

"Don't fret. I have enough faith for the both of us."

Waving a hand in dismissal, Fara shook her head. "Just come on. Let's get this over with."

They'd arrived at a small market at the base of the main climb to the Mist Knights' castle and training grounds and tournament arena. Banners painted to show the various mountain dragon subspecies fluttered from poles. Most of the banners showed the massive Heartsworns with their scarlet scales while a few held images of the vicious and blood-thirsty Green-flanked Terrors. Banners with Spikebacks the color of the clouds and sky stood to the right. Some displayed Speedy Seabreaks with their four ocean-blue wings. Leather bags and belts lay stacked on tables and jugs of wine and mead lined a stall under a pale green awning. Merchants hawked their wares with their impressively loud voices. Mist Fae like Fara could truly shout if they wanted to. Tahlia really hoped that didn't come up during the tournament. Younglings ran underfoot through the market, bumping into fist-waving old males and jostling customers with items clutched in their arms. Across the chaos, a table laden with tourney leathers sat like a big, fat present for Tahlia.

"Come on." Tahlia urged the mare to hurry.

Fara came up beside her. She was licking her lips and had one hand on her stomach. "I would beat someone to nothing for a bite of those meat pies." Her hunger was legendary.

"We should have some coin left after this. I think. Maybe." Tahlia gave Fara a look that was half grimace, half smile.

"If you let me do the bartering."

Tahlia shook her head. "Not a chance. Your cute joke about beatings will turn into reality. Your job is to mind the mare." She handed her the reins as they approached the table.

The merchant's back was to them, his blue skin shining in the golden light that passed through the airy mist. "Do you have the coin for this?" he barked out. "If not, don't waste my time."

"We do."

He turned and looked Tahlia up and down. "How about you meet me for a drink at sundown instead? You're only going to get your little self killed in that tournament."

Fara lurched forward, the veins in her neck and forehead standing out. Tahlia put a hand on her wrist and kept her voice calm.

"Thanks for the offer, but I'm ridiculously determined," Tahlia said.

"Ridiculous is accurate. Well, at least you're aware of it. That'll be forty-nine gladecoins." He produced a string marked with black lines here and there and proceeded to lean over his wares to measure her torso and waist lazily.

Tahlia raised an eyebrow. "Take your time."

"It's not easy over this table with you so small and everything. You're lucky your chest isn't overly sumptuous."

"Gee, thanks."

Fara snorted and Tahlia elbowed her roughly, though she couldn't help but snicker.

The merchant went into a tent behind his table, then appeared again with leathers in tow. He shoved a vest, a helmet, and trousers. She handed over the coin and a thrill hit her chest.

"It's happening," she whispered as she dragged Fara behind a stall with a black awning and curtain to try on the purchase.

"It is whether I like it or not. Do we have enough for food or did you give it all away? I'm absolutely starving." Fara's stomach growled and she lifted her eyebrows as if to say, *See?*

Tahlia wrangled the vest over her head and Fara began jerking the tough leather into place. The vest snared on Tahlia's shoulder.

Fara snorted. "Fits perfectly." She growled and pulled harder.

"Hey, easy there," Tahlia grunted out. "I may not have a lot going on in the chest vicinity, but what I do have, I'd like to keep intact."

By the time they had it on and laced, they were both red-cheeked and laughing. Tahlia worked off her boots and put on the trousers. They didn't fit well—big and small in all the wrong places—but they would do. She replaced her boots, and then held out her arms for Fara to examine her.

Fara stood back and crossed her arms. "You look the part at least. Well, you're too short to appear threatening, but other than that, I'm impressed at what an outfit can do."

Tahlia spun with her arms wide. "I am never taking it off."

Fara dragged her toward a table where a fellow with orange skin was selling meat pies. "Two please," Fara said to the pie seller. She turned to Tahlia. "Do you want one?"

"You ordered two," Tahlia said.

"One for this side of my stomach and one for the other."

"Three please," Tahlia said to the male.

The male handed out the pies. "You competing this go around?"

Fara had one unwrapped and half eaten before Tahlia could blink. "No," Fara said through her mouthful, "she's just wearing the outfit because it's so comfy."

The merchant ignored Fara's sarcasm. "You don't have a pound to spare, lass. Sure you can handle a dragon? You must have Mistgold blood so bright it burns the Bloodworker's eyes."

Tahlia swallowed around a lump in her throat. "Definitely. Yep. Loads of gold in these veins." She set her jaw and stared back at the merchant, attempting to ooze confidence. It gave her an immediate headache.

"Aye, I see that ferocity in your eyes. Hope it's enough!"

"Thank you." Tahlia turned away and headed toward the Mist Road.

Fara caught up, crumbs falling as she walked.

"We need to focus now," Tahlia said. "Maybe go over my backstory and yours."

"Mine can stay what it is," Fara said.

Fara was a full Fae and had grown up not an hour's walk from here, so she was likely right except for one thing.

"What about your mother?" Tahlia asked.

"I'll use a different surname."

Tahlia tucked her pie into the small bag tied to her belt to save for later. "She won't show up to watch the tournament, right?"

"No way." Fara licked her fingers. "She's too old for that now. Has to be."

"You don't sound one hundred percent positive."

"I am no Seer."

"Good enough. Now, I am Lady Tahlia of Northwoods. I'll keep most of mine the same so we don't have too much to remember. One brother. Left Northwoods to gain work as a squire even though my brother was against it. I might have to claim that both of my parents fell out of favor and died years ago."

"Smart," Fara said around a mouthful. "That way they won't be encouraged to figure out if they have met your kin at court or area festivals. What are you going to say of your experience with dragons? You know they will have a Mist Knight interview you. It is a casual affair from what I've heard, but those folks don't miss much."

"I'll just claim I was at Grimsbrook for six years."

The mare tossed her head at the increasing steepness of the path. Tahlia rubbed her neck and whispered encouragement to Daffodil as Grimsbrook passed through her mind.

The period when Tahlia had trained at that old keep during her thirteenth year had been tough. The dragons though—they had been amazing. Tahlia had taken right to riding, but the other Fae in attendance had bullied her to the extreme. After a few broken ribs and a knockout that made her forget her name for a full day, her mother had pulled her out of the academy. She'd only been there for six months. If she were there now, she would fight them, but she had been young and small for her age.

Fara wiped her mouth with the back of her hand and folded the meat pie parchment. "Do you have a family sigil to use when you sign the book?" She put the parchment in her trouser pocket and rubbed her greasy hands on her knees.

"I'll use a tree and a dragon's tooth as a sigil. It's common enough that I can blend in, right?"

"You're the boss," Fara said.

"No, we are a team."

Fara stopped. "No, Lady Tahlia. At this point, I need to be seen as your squire." She reached for the reins. "Now, give me these."

Tahlia released her hold and chewed her lip. "All right. That's probably for the best. Promise you don't think I'm an arrogant witch?"

Fara led Daffodil ahead. "Oh, you are, but that's what it takes to ride dragons."

True. She grinned at Fara's back. The Old Ones had certainly blessed her with a good friend.

After a half hour of walking the punishing incline through the wet, cold clouds of the Mist Road, the gate of the Mist Knights' castle rose like a stone giant crowned in sparkling gold and blue crystals the size of Tahlia's arm. The crystals were the reason the dragons lived in these mountains—they gave the creatures power and strength.

"Tourney competitor?" a voice said through the mist.

They continued on a step and the mist cleared enough to see the two males in Mist Knight livery— black and blue crystalline shapes surrounding a dragon with wings spread across the guards' chests.

"Yes. I'm competing." Tahlia impressed herself by not allowing her words to shake.

"Good luck, dragon rider." The other guard swung one of the double doors wide.

A shiver ran from Tahlia's head to her toes. Her heart beat double time. "Thank you."

Fara was grinning at her as they entered the outer bailey of the Mist Knights' home, the place Tahlia had dreamed about her entire life.

CHAPTER 5
MARIUS

At the end of the tournament grounds, Marius dismounted and walked around to Ragewing's head. The dragon trilled and Marius rubbed the beast between the eyes, then under the chin. The smooth warmth of Ragewing's scales and the scent of the dragon's fire-smoke breath loosened the tightness in Marius's shoulders and neck. Ragewing's flame-like eyes studied Marius, intelligence flickering in their depths. The dragon snuffled against Marius's scar, the one that ran all the way from hairline to chin on the left side of his face.

"It doesn't bother me anymore. I swear it."

Ragewing tucked him under a wing and the creature's protectiveness warmed Marius's heart.

"You did very well today, Ragewing. As usual." He ran both hands down the dragon's lower neck and chest, then began loosening the girth. "I don't want to head back to the stables at the moment, friend. It'll be packed with everyone rubbing down their mounts. Plus those noisy younglings your sister just bore..."

Raising his snout to the air, Ragewing let out a low, proud growl.

"You are such the doting uncle, hmm?" Marius smiled and rolled up the dirtied linen he'd used on the dragon's scales and tossed it into the laundry bin.

The quiet here on the far side of the stands was pleasant and the angle of the wall created a nice shelter from the wind. He could see the grounds and the open gate at the other end, and perhaps was less noticeable—although hiding with a dragon was near to impossible. He was so tired of answering tournament questions. Yesterday, everyone and their mother had been querying him about how many competitors would be in this year's event, what the chances were of someone dying, and who was the favorite. The enthusiasm of the newer knights was commendable, but he wished the commander or even Ophelia would speak up more often. He pushed his worries away and worked on Ragewing's tail and feet, removing debris and applying dabs of the herbal unguent he kept in a small leather-wrapped vial in his belt bag.

A female with tan skin and wavy, shoulder-length dark hair strode into the arena, her head swiveling and her eyes wide. If he didn't know better, he'd have guessed she was here to watch, but she wore a set of ridiculously out-of-date riding leathers. She must be a competitor in the tournament. She spun, her arms wide, and a laugh like chimes rang from her mouth. His lips lifted. Most competitors were far too terrified to enjoy the beauty and majesty of the tourney grounds or to show such joy at simply being here. But fear was the wiser reaction. Stopping mid-spin, the female stared in his direction. He and Ragewing had been spotted.

Marius growled. "Oh, goodie. More questions."

Ragewing bumped his shoulder.

"I'll be polite," he whispered, "but she needs to be informed of the danger. Obviously she is clueless. And quite small for this task."

"Good morning," she said, her voice bright as she approached.

Her eyes were a dark golden brown, like the honey gathered in the valley at the base of the mountains. She was incredibly petite, barely reaching the midpoint of Ragewing's foreleg. Her gaze slid over his face and body. He swallowed. What was she thinking?

She eyed Ragewing, full lips parting as she studied his tucked wings and the two spikes on his head.

Marius bowed shallowly. "Morning. I assume you plan to compete for the new Mist Knight position?" Her uniform was actually a set of mock leathers some of the market merchants sold to children. He didn't think she knew that.

"Yes." She set her slender hands on her stomach, then patted herself down. "Is there something wrong with my armor?"

He gritted his teeth. She'd be seriously injured wearing those ratty, ill-fitting strips of poor material. "Don't you have a sponsor?"

"I am independent."

Of course she was. Serious contenders took the time to find noble families that would team up with the dragon rider's kin to pay for gear. Fighting the urge to shake his head, he blew out a frustrated breath. "If you pass the interview and blood test, then I will see to it you receive proper gear."

She'd fisted her hands at his mention of the

steps to enter the tournament, but now her face cleared and she smiled like a sunrise. "Really? You'd do that for me? You are so kind! I bet you're really highly ranked what with your purple tassels and all. You must know High Captain Marius." Coming close, she leaned toward him and eyed the arena. "Is he as tough as they say?"

He pressed his eyes shut. There wasn't enough patience in the world...

A squawking sounded and suddenly a youngling dragon barreled across the arena. Ragewing launched himself toward his nephew by blood. The female Fae's eyes widened and she ran—surprisingly quickly—toward the youngling, getting between the dragons. Marius's heart shot into his throat and his head pounded as he sprinted to catch up.

She held out her arms and spoke up to Ragewing. "He's not intending to threaten your rider."

"Back away," Marius commanded. "Ragewing, she means no harm. Back away!" he shouted at the female. "That youngling is his kin."

The female glanced at Marius, then slowly moved away from the dragons. Ragewing loped forward and set his wing over the yowling young beast.

"Aww, look at them." The female was grinning and had her fists tucked under her chin like she was witnessing the most wonderful thing in the world.

Ragewing licked the youngling's head, cleaning the small dragon as if he were his own. It was rather adorable, but also dangerous.

"You could have been killed," Marius said to the female. "That was incredibly reckless."

"There's no need to shout at me. I realize I made a mistake. Is this how the High Captain trains you to respond when someone is trying to help? No wonder everyone is scared of him."

He stared, waiting for her to figure it out. She was the most infuriating person he had ever met.

Her gaze slid to the whip curled around his shoulder, then her fingers flew to her full rosy lips and her cheeks pinked.

Warmth coiled low in his body and he cleared his throat.

"Old Ones save me," she whispered. "You *are* the High Captain!"

Inclining his head slightly, he glared. "Indeed."

Shadows had bloomed across the arena, and a dark-haired, purple-skinned female leading a horse walked up to the south entrance of the arena. It was past time to finish this and get Ragewing back to his stall.

"I... I didn't realize..." she stammered.

For the first time, she seemed at a loss for words. A miracle.

"And you are late to the sign-ups," he said tightly. "Is that your squire? You must turn in your vial of blood immediately."

"Thank you. Yes." She gave him a grin and bow, then ran to meet up with the other female that he assumed was her squire. They hurried out of the arena, horse in tow.

At least she had listened to his warning about time. Foolish thing.

He ran a hand down Ragewing's shoulder. "Surely, she won't make it past the interview. We can't let more of these fools enter and get themselves killed. Some just do not have the proper respect for our work..." Grumbling, he tried to focus on herding Ragewing and the youngling back toward the stables, but the female with the dark honey eyes and the pink cheeks never really left his thoughts.

CHAPTER 6

TAHLIA

igh Captain Marius Leos Valentius. She had actually met him. Spoken to him. A stuttered breath left her. Just with his gaze, he'd given her lovely shivers.

"I lost you at the bend in the road." Irritation clipped Fara's words.

Tahlia held up a hand. She hadn't meant to worry her friend. This place was just so incredible that she could hardly focus on doing anything. The sights and sounds and smells drew her attention back and forth and around again like she was watching a pitchball game.

"I'm sorry. I noticed the arena and just had to see it for myself immediately."

A reluctant grin crossed Fara's mouth. "Fine."

"Did you ask what we need at the sign-up table?" Tahlia asked. "I assume you found it past that crowd?"

"I did. They want your blood for the test right now and they say if we don't have it turned in by the next bell, you can't compete."

A grimace tugged at Tahlia's mouth. "I had no idea there was a time limit."

"Where are we doing this?" Fara was already fingering the hilt of her dagger.

Tahlia dug around in the bag strewn across her body. There had to be a bottle in here somewhere.

"How about over there?" she whispered.

Fara curled her lip. "Near the public piss pots?"

Finally, a cool, curved item touched Tahlia's fingertips. She drew out a green vial, one that their former employer used to gather seeds of medicinal plants. "Yes, come on."

She dragged Fara into one of the curtained toilet tents, leaving Daffodil chomping on a clump of weeds outside. Thankfully, this particular tent was empty. Uncorking the bottle with her teeth, Tahlia let loose a horrible groan.

Fara's eyes went wide. "What is your problem?"

"If everyone thinks someone is sick in here, they'll leave us alone."

Nodding, Fara pursed her lips and gave a cough and a groan too.

Knocking the rest of the seeds from the vial, Tahlia grinned. "That's the spirit."

Fara used her dagger to make a small cut about halfway up her arm and Tahlia held the bottle up against the wound. Fara's Mistgold Fae blood flowed into the vial.

Tahlia found a bandage at the bottom of the sack and helped Fara tidy up her arm and roll her sleeve back down. Tahlia took Fara's face between her hands.

"Thank you for doing this."

Fara grinned, her cheeks puffing around Tahlia's fingers. "Just don't die on me."

"I'll do my best to live on and annoy you forever."

Back at the sign-up table, Tahlia handed the vial over to a barrel-chested, blue-skinned male. "My blood sample." She gave him what she hoped was a winning smile as her heart rate increased and her hands grew clammy.

His features held no emotion. He took the offered bottle and set it beside a long sheet of parchment. "Name?"

"Lady Tahlia of Northwoods."

"Experience in years?"

"With dragons?"

His gaze snapped to her face and he just stared.

"Oh, of course." A nervous laugh bubbled from her. "Six years at Grimsbrook."

The male's grip tightened on his red feather quill. "Really?" He looked her up and down.

She tugged at her leather vest and raised her chin defiantly. She was so lucky the human half of her allowed her to lie. "Yes."

He jerked his head in a nod and inked her name onto the parchment. "Sigil?"

"Tree and dragon tooth."

Waving a hand to indicate he needed more detail than that, he paused in writing.

"The tooth sits longwise above an oak's silhouette."

"Ah." He jotted down some unreadable notes, then set his quill down and cracked his knuckles. "Your interview will be at the Brass Lantern with High Captain Marius." He handed her a scroll shut with a waxed blue and silver seal.

"But..."

"You're lucky. With that level of experience, you will have plenty to discuss with him."

Tahlia's neck heated and she gripped the tiny scroll tightly. "Of course. Yes. Thank you. What time?"

"At sundown. You can eat together if he is in the right mood."

Fara leaned over Tahlia's shoulder. "Right mood?"

Tahlia imagined that Marius would be in a foul mood considering he didn't agree with how she behaved with the youngling dragon. But she would win him over. Somehow.

The male chuckled knowingly. "You'll see." He shooed them on and began asking the male behind them the entry questions.

Fara urged the horse around a cluster of children trading painted stones. "You didn't ask when we'll hear the results of the blood test?"

"I am sure they'll let us know at the interview if there was any issue, which there won't be." Each of the children's stones had a sigil on it, perhaps of their favorite knight or dragon...

"It's nearly sundown now. Tell me about that knight in the arena."

They walked the winding path that wound

through a market and along the higher cliffs that stretched into the peachy late-afternoon sky. Stairs ran along the cliffs and numerous Fae walked here and there. They lived in the caves carved from the mountain's face and each cave boasted a crystal above its arched entrance.

"It was the High Captain." Tahlia grimaced at Fara.

Fara gripped Tahlia's arm. "What?"

"Yes, I didn't recognize him. He seemed too young to be the male everyone talks about." And too good looking. That whip on his shoulder made her mind whirl with thoughts that were decidedly unknightlike...

Fara's grip on Tahlia's arm went slack. "We are as good as dead."

"Why?"

"Because." Fara shoved her hands in her hair and turned in a circle. "Now he knows your face and you didn't know who he was. A terrible first impression. He'll know you're sneaking in here," she whispered in a hiss, "and that your blood is false and he'll come looking for us and will have his dragon roast us for his supper."

"Fara."

"I don't want to be someone's supper." Fara's

eyes were wild—a sure sign of her losing it. "I want to have a meal, not be one!"

Tahlia grabbed her by the arms and stared her in the face. "Fara. You must stop yelling." *Especially yelling about our secrets,* she tried to say with her eyes.

Fara's gaze took in the crowd around them. "Right."

"But you didn't let me tell you the best part," Tahlia whispered as the crowd stopped paying them any attention. "He was tending to Ragewing. That dragon is glorious. The colors, the scales, the fire-bright eyes... And High Captain Marius wasn't too bad himself with his immense height and that fierce stare. He has this powerful presence..."

"Yes, yes. Attractive and dangerous male. Just every idiot's type. Now, can we go find our lodgings?"

Tahlia leaned close. "We don't have the money for that."

"They provide lodging to those who have one of those." Fara jerked her chin toward Tahlia's hand—where the small scroll was gripped in her fingers.

"Ah. All right." The street branched out, and down at the end of the western route, an archway made entirely of crystal sparkled above the crowd.

"I'm guessing that is the entrance to the inner bailey."

The crowd thinned as they approached the archway and one of the four guards in Mist Knight livery standing at the entrance raised his sword.

"I swear on the Old Ones' greatest crystal," the guard shouted at the gathered folk. "If you don't back up, I'll lop the heads from the lot of you!"

"Calm down, Severin. They're just excited," another guard said.

"Only competitors! No rabble!" Severin said, glaring at the people straining their necks to see through the arch.

The second, more level-headed guard shook his head and waved Tahlia forward. "You have your mark?"

She held up the tiny scroll. "You mean this?"

He took it, cracked the seal, and read it over. "Yep. You're in. This your squire, yes?" He was looking behind her at Fara.

"Yes. Where do I find our lodgings?"

"Straight through there." He pointed down a side street inside the archway. "A stable hand will take your horse at that second archway. Then you'll come to an unmarked door where competitor lodgings are given out. Remember, be on your best behavior. There is always a dragon watching the castle." His smile was sharp. He elbowed her. "Just kidding you, knight. Get on in there and make your hometown proud!"

Tahlia's heart thudded and her smile turned absolutely feral. She was more than ready to do just that. Fara shut her eyes—she was probably praying —and they passed into the legendary castle of the Mist Knights, the very heart of the Shrouded Mountains.

CHAPTER 7
TAHLIA

Fara paced the chamber the Mist Knight's servant had given them for lodging during the two-day tournament. "I hope Daffodil isn't stabled beside a dragon."

Tahlia gave her a look from where she lounged on the bed by the door. "They know we didn't bring her as a midnight snack."

A strangled noise came from Fara. "I can't believe you're going to jump onto a dragon tomorrow! Are you certain about this? Can't we just set up a nice little table here and sell arts and crafts?"

"You've never made anything crafty in your entire life."

"That's beside the point."

"It isn't."

"No, but Mist Knights can be cruel. They test you when you're up there," Fara said, pointing at the ceiling but presumably meaning the sky, "and if you fall, they will just let you die. Ack! I'd forgotten! You met the High Captain! Tell me everything. Was he covered in blood?"

"Stars, Fara, no, he wasn't coming back from war."

"You don't know that."

"I doubt they'd be holding a tournament if we were suddenly at war."

"Fine. Now, how did he act?"

"Polite. His dragon was amazing. And his dragon's nephew made an appearance. Cutest thing I've ever seen."

"Did he scold you for being in the arena without permission?"

"The dragon?"

Fara's nostrils flared, so Tahlia ceased the teasing.

"He was a touch grouchy looking but he didn't say anything negative," Tahlia said, the High Captain's storm-gray eyes and deep, stony voice flashing through her mind. "Maybe his face is just like that."

Fara lifted the blanket on the bed and examined the sheets underneath. It was her usual spider check.

"He said if I pass the interview," Tahlia continued, "he would find me some better riding leathers."

Dropping her bag on the bed, Fara spun. "He what?"

"And the fact that he is the one assigned to give me the interview, I bet I'll have a brand-new set by tomorrow morning."

"You actually feel good about him interviewing you? I'd be a puddle of fear on the floor. Plus, you didn't recognize him at first, right? He has to be irritated."

"There's more chance he is annoyed with the way I slipped between his dragon and the youngling dragon."

"What?" Fara looked ready to keel over.

"It's okay. I put myself between his dragon and the youngling because I was afraid the big guy was going to attack him. The youngling was running straight at the High Captain."

"You did what?"

"Your voice is doing that squealy thing again."

Making claws of her fingers, Fara glared.

"I was trying to help and the High Captain didn't

think that was a good idea. But he knew the youngling was his dragon's nephew and I didn't. An honest mistake."

"You got between the dragons? Seriously? That wasn't some sort of slang idiom I am not aware of? Like 'oh, today I was between the dragons. It was a hellish afternoon.'"

"No. Not an idiom."

Fara covered her face with her hands. "We are doomed."

"I choose to believe he isn't mad at me. He isn't that horrible. He was gentle with his dragon and I think he's a good person. Truly. Maybe everyone just believes he is cruel because of his grouchy face."

"But what about the high number of foes he has killed and the great number of knights-in-training that he has kicked out of the castle?" Fara asked.

Tahlia shrugged. "We don't know what stories are true."

"I wonder if that one about him chasing a stable hand off the mountain with his whip is true."

"I doubt that. He could probably have scared the fellow away with just his glare."

Fara laughed, her shoulders relaxing away from her ears a bit. "What are you going to wear to the interview?"

"Not this?" Tahlia patted her leathers.

"You are supposed to wear civilian clothing, I believe."

"I'll see what I can do with our lady's green trousers and that scarlet tunic of hers."

Nodding, Fara pulled them from the saddlebag. "I'll shake them out and smooth them as best I can while you go to the baths."

"Ooooh, the baths."

"I've heard they are the best in the land besides King Lysanael's."

Thoughts of hot steam and lavender-scented soaps were already making Tahlia swoon.

Fara grabbed her arm before she could leave. "But be careful. You must go to the trainees' bathing area, not the knights' area."

"Or I'll be in hot water?" Tahlia wiggled her eyebrows.

Fara rolled her eyes. "Go on."

Tahlia whistled as she left the chamber and headed down the corridor. There was only one way to go, as the corridor dead-ended the other direction. At a fork, a chalked sign hung from the ceiling. One arrow was marked GREAT HALL and the other said BATHING CHAMBERS. Simple enough.

The bathing area's high ceiling let in the sunset's

orange glow. A few males and females walked this way and that, mostly wrapped in bathing sheets and carrying folded stacks of clothing. Some had tall cups of something that smelled like mint. Multiple rooms branched off of the main area, and without signs, she had to guess which one was for her.

Tahlia ended up in a smaller room with a deep circular pool of steaming water and a set of shelves stocked with sheets as well as a pitcher and three of those tall cups. Had there been a sign as to who was supposed to use this bathing room and she had just missed it? She went back to the arch she'd passed through but didn't see a sign anywhere.

Well, no one was here anyway, so it had to be fine. She set to peeling off her road-stained clothing and boots. Three steps led into the water, and the feel of its heat was dream-worthy. Sinking all the way in, she let the water cover her head. It was incredible. She was in good shape and could handle a lot, but that climb up the mountain had made her muscles sore. The hot water loosened them up and helped her relax.

Everything was going to be wonderful. She'd be clean and ready to meet the High Captain after this. In fact, she'd be so nicely tidied up that he probably wouldn't remember seeing her covered in road dust in the arena. Yes, she would get a chance at a better first impression.

Rising up out of the water, she ran her hands over her hair to slick the moisture out. She opened her eyes and lost the ability to move.

High Captain Marius stood at the far end of the bath.

His hair was fully wet as if he too had been underwater. Droplets fell from his strong brow to black and gold inkings that curled across his large chest muscles. The inking snaked down his wet side to his hipbone and further, though the water obscured the rest. Inkings were for those who had suffered a great loss. Who had he lost?

Her heart was a ringing bell in her ears. She lifted her gaze, cheeks blazing like a thousand dragons aimed their fire right at her. A lovely heat gathered low in her belly. "I'm guessing *I'm* the one in the wrong chamber."

The corner of his lips twitched as if he almost wanted to laugh but his eyes said he was too irritated to give in. His gaze never strayed from her face. "You certainly are."

"I..." She swam toward the stairs and he stepped

fully into the deeper center of the pool, avoiding her. "I'm sorry. I'll go now." A laugh bubbled inside her, but she fought it back as she glanced at his scowl once more. "Feel free to enjoy the show," she joked, "but if you want to turn around, I'll grab my clothes."

Facing the shelving, she heard the water moving around him. Was he turning around? Why wasn't he saying anything? Had she really upset him that badly?

Quickly, she dried and dressed. Heading for the archway, she looked his way. He stared at the wall opposite the shelves, his gorgeously muscled back to her.

"Sorry again!" A chuckle bounced out of her before she could exit the area. As soon as she was in the main bathing chamber, her snickering turned into a full belly laugh. Only she would end up naked with the legendary dragon rider within hours of arriving in the Shrouded Mountains.

"Control yourself, competitor." A female with blue-green hair and blue eyes glared down at Tahlia. Her thin but strong-looking arms were crossed and she wore the full regalia of a high-ranking dragon rider, just as the High Captain had in the arena. Small purple tassels hung from the shoulders of her white leathers, and a wreath of golden laurel leaves wove through her tightly braided hair.

"Laughing is not allowed?" Tahlia twisted her hair and squeezed water from the ends.

The female's nose wrinkled and she stepped back. "Buffoonery isn't a characteristic of a Mist Knight. You'll learn soon enough who does and who does not belong." Her gaze cut Tahlia before she marched away and joined a group of three half-dressed females standing in front of another steaming chamber.

Tahlia smiled at the female's retreating figure. "I belong. Don't worry." She said it more to herself than anyone.

The female whirled and glared for a moment before going back to her associates.

"Could you maybe tell me which chamber I am supposed to use?"

The females continued their chat and ignored her question. Shrugging them off, Tahlia strode past the group and entered the chamber they seemed to be claiming. Several females bathed in the pool and a few were dressing by a torch-lit alcove. They had riding leathers, but no fancy tassels or wreaths of honor.

"Are you my fellow competitors?"

"We are." One of the females in the water nodded.

There was no more talk as Tahlia finished the washing she'd started in the high-ranking male chamber. *Guess that's another rule.* The list in her head was getting quite long...

CHAPTER 8
TAHLIA

The Brass Lantern stood in the outer bailey of the castle among the houses and shops of the common folk and craftsfae. Though the sign looked ready to drop from age, the inside was rather pleasant. A fire crackled on one side of the large main room and tables in all shapes and sizes sat in clusters to create a pathway for the servers bringing trays of food and drink. Everything smelled delightfully of bread.

Tahlia had no time for bread at the moment though—stones, wasn't that a sad thought? Bread was the stuff of dreams. But so was seeing the High Captain and his inkings in the bathing chamber.

She tugged at the neckline of her tunic. "Is it overly warm in here?"

"I don't think so. I'm freezing. As usual." Fara eyed her. "You're red. What's wrong? Are you sick? Was anyone coughing in the bathing chamber? I've heard there is an ague going around. I'll go get you an herbal tea. My grandmother used to say—"

Tahlia snagged her arm. "Fara. Breathe. I'm not sick. Just...nervous." She hadn't told her friend about the wonderfully horrible mistake in the bathing chambers. Fara would have exploded from fret. "I'm fine."

But what would Marius say about the fact that she had seen him naked from the waist up? And why was she thinking of him as Marius? It was a nice name though. Just as nice as the way that water had slid down his body to that place near his hip... A shuddering breath left her.

"He isn't here," Fara said over Tahlia's shoulder. "I wonder if they know about the blood. They've found you out," she whispered.

Tahlia waved her worry away. "Don't catastrophize. He's here somewhere. If they had discovered our secret, the mountain guard would already be dragging me to prison or whatever horrible thing you were afraid of."

"You might think your little pep talk is helpful, but I assure you, it is not."

In the far corner behind a group of green-skinned males who all had the same nose shape, Marius sat at a table alone. His brow furrowed as he read through a stack of parchment. He grabbed a small scarlet book beside the stack and scribbled something inside. His quill bobbed and he paused to touch his chin as if in deep thought. The light of the tavern's sconces, candles, and fire drew out shining lines of gold in his moon-white hair. He'd pulled it back into a queue.

Tahlia took an unsteady breath. He was really far too lovely to be scary. Even the scar that ran all the way down his face worked to make him alluring. "I see him."

"Uh, yeah, I can tell you do."

Tahlia whipped around to look at Fara, who was grinning.

"Don't let him muddle your mind, Tahlia. He may be as hot as his dragon's fire, but he is also just as dangerous considering the trick you've played on him and his associates to get here."

"I'll be smart. Try to stop worrying."

"Sure. Next I'll stop my heart from beating. No problem."

Tahlia chuckled. Giving her friend a quick tap on

the arm, she walked away and toward Marius's table.

He looked up as she approached and his stern expression faltered, lips parting slightly and eyes widening a fraction. "You?"

Oh, he hadn't known he was assigned to her. Should she apologize for barging in on his bath? Or just let it be and forget it happened? His expression showed contempt. He hated her. She'd have to change that.

"Yes, me," she said. "I hope they gave you all the potential competitors' information there." Glancing at the parchments and book, Tahlia slid into the chair across from him, folded her arms on the table, and smiled as she looked into his storm-gray eyes. "I'm thrilled to have been assigned to you for my interview."

"You shouldn't be. I'm the toughest interviewer on the mountain."

And the best looking in the baths. Swallowing, she cleared her throat. "Well, what would you like to know?"

"I'll be the one asking questions."

"Of course, sir. As you wish."

He sifted through his parchment until he found

what he was looking for and held it aloft. "Potential competitor five. Hmm."

With a grunt, he studied the written lines. He looked like someone had poked him with a sharp stick. What did that *hmm* mean?

"The committee," he said with that gravelly voice of his, "states here that you spent years at Grimsbrook."

"I did."

His gaze whipped across her face. "Say that in full, please."

He wanted her Fae blood to stop any deceit from spilling from her lips. But he didn't know she was half-human and could lie fairly well.

Meeting his gaze, she said, "I trained at Grimsbrook for six years."

Blinking and nodding, he went back to his page. "What sub-breeds did you work with there?"

She had worked with several kinds even though she'd only been at Grimsbrook for a short time. Most of what she knew of dragons, she'd learned from books and scrolls.

"Green-flanked Terrors, for one," she said.

"What did you learn about the greens?"

What did he want to hear? "They eat twice as

much if you let them, but they don't need that much to be healthy. Their flame travels farther than any other breed's. They were originally nocturnal and are prone to eye strain, so they work better longer if given protracticol before a day flight."

"What are the risks involved with that concoction?"

"Lethargy if given too much. And addiction. They enjoy the feel of the herbs in their bloodstream."

He set both hands on the table. They were easily twice the size of hers. For the thousandth time, she wished she were bigger. It would make riding easier and would keep so many from underestimating her.

"Tell me about another sub-breed you rode at Grimsbrook."

"I rode a Heartsworn that was a bit smaller than your dragon." She waited for him to comment, but he remained silent. She cleared her throat. "She didn't want me on her back because Heartsworns are loyal to a fault and she was bonded with a male there. I wore his cloak to give her his scent, but she bucked me off almost immediately." Maybe she shouldn't have told him that. "I also rode a Spike-back and used its shorter bursts of fire in close sparring."

Cocking his head to the side, he studied her face. Was he about to order her to leave the mountain? Was it over already?

"What would you command your dragon to do if you were surrounded by three enemy dragons and their riders?"

The questions went on and on from there until Tahlia's stomach was growling with hunger. She coughed to cover the sound and prayed this interview would end before she died of starvation. The whole tavern smelled like bread and meat and it was such a torture. Fara would have already perished.

"Well, you do know your dragons," Marius said. His voice was powerful even at this low volume. It was obvious that he had Mistgold to spare in his blood. "Now, tell me," he commanded. "Why do you want to do this? Why leave a safe life on the ground for one in the sky surrounded by fire and pirates' iron?"

Tahlia's heart lifted and thudded in her ears. "I wouldn't be who I am if I chose the safer route in life. Flying on dragonback is the only time I truly feel like myself."

A smile tugged at one side of his mouth, the most she'd seen of a happy expression in the male. Warmth filled her chest and ran up into her cheeks. It was fun getting him to let go of that sternness. Plus it was an interesting challenge trying to please someone so steely and generally disgruntled.

"As soon as I get the approval from the Bloodworkers," he said, "I will put your name in for the lists."

Squeezing her hands in her lap to keep from leaping up like a maniac to celebrate, she listened to his list of questions concerning Fara's squire-like qualities as well as inquiries as to what skills Tahlia had besides riding.

"And what weapon do you choose on the ground?" he asked.

"The gladius."

His glance hooked her sharply. "A longer sword would be better for one as short-limbed as you."

Tahlia pursed her lips. "I'm pretty good with it."

He nodded and jotted the word down under her name in his scarlet book. Was that his personal record of competitors or was that some official book?

"In the sky?"

"Bow."

"Have you tried a whip?"

Her gaze went to his shoulder. His whip was no

longer curled there, but she remembered its tidy braid and the sheen of the well-oiled leather.

"I haven't. Will you teach me? That would be amazing."

"No, I don't have time. You don't have the luxury of additional training either. The events will begin at dawn tomorrow with the Presentation of the Competitors, and I have word King Lysanael and Queen Revna will be in attendance. After that, you will be tested on ground weapons and flying. A short break will be provided in the early afternoon before the mock sky battle. If you are still alive at that point, you will be required to attend the announcement of the one who has earned the open position."

"I can't wait."

"That answer only shows ignorance."

"I'm not supposed to be excited about the tournament?"

"It's a deadly challenge. Some don't make it through."

"No one has died in the tournament in years. Actually, none that I've heard about since you were given your current rank." He might have seemed cold, but he ran a good show here, if the stats were any indication.

He waved off her attempt at subtle praise. "You

should temper your joy. It will make you reckless in the clouds. I know. I've seen it."

"Temper your joy. You're even worse at pep talks than me." Tahlia couldn't help herself; she chuckled.

Marius just glared.

"High Captain?" A male in Mist Knight livery bowed beside the table.

"Yes?"

"I have blood test results you should see."

Tahlia's veins ran with ice. This was it. Would her and Fara's trick fly?

"Thank you," Marius said as he took a sealed scroll from the messenger.

The seal was the same blue as the livery, but the image in the wax showed a whip and a crystal—had to be Marius's sigil.

"Don't you use your family's sigil? Did your father or mother also use the whip?"

"I chose my own sigil when I arrived here."

"But why not carry on your family's sigil?"

"Has anyone ever told you that it's rude to pry into people's pasts?"

"They have tried." She grinned and tried to make that glare fade. No such luck. "Sorry. I'll let you keep your secrets."

"I doubt you've kept a secret your entire life."

"You don't know me."

He cracked the seal but kept his stormy gaze on her. "I know you are intelligent, reckless, and you run your pretty lips like a drunken bard playing a lute."

Pretty? Her face went hot.

Sniffing, he focused on the scroll's contents. Someone with a lantern passed by the outside window and their light spread over Marius's throat and his upper chest where his shirt gaped a little. A curve of his inking showed.

Marius frowned and she dragged her gaze away from the smooth skin of his upper chest.

"Do you want to know what the Bloodworkers say of your blood?" he asked.

She held very still. "Yes."

"You have a high rating of Mistgold in your veins as well as a hint of human."

Her jaw unclenched and she took a full breath. Thank the Old Ones.

"You must come from an old line of dragon riders," he continued, "because no one up here has a human in their ancestry."

Fara's blood showed she had at least one human ancestor? Tahlia didn't think her friend knew that. Now, if the workers had been studying Tahlia's blood in truth, they'd have seen basically no Mist-gold and a load of human ancestry...

Nodding, she tried to appear confident. She relaxed her hands on the table and leaned back. "I don't know of any humans, but I suppose someone could have kept it secret."

"It's certainly nothing to be proud of."

"Humans aren't that bad."

"Aren't they?"

"The queen is a great ruler." It had been a shock when King Lysanael had married and mated with the human, but it was so far, so good with her on the throne.

"True," Marius said, "but she is an exception."

"How many humans have you known?"

Why was she arguing? She needed to shut her mouth and end this thing as quickly as possible before she messed up.

Marius's nostrils flared. "We're finished here. I know what I need to know."

Her pulse stamped against her neck like an impatient horse. Holding her tongue was more difficult than her moments spent on that Heartsworn's back.

"I should fail you," he said. "I should save your life."

"You don't think I can do this." She realized she had leaned forward and was fisting her hands on the table. Relaxing her fingers, she tried to slow her breathing.

"I do not. You are too small, too rash around dragons, and ignorant of the risks in the life you are attempting to begin."

"But you said *should*. That you *should fail* me. That means you are only considering it."

"The most important trait for a dragon rider is courage. If you prove that you aren't as ignorant of the risks, then you might be the bravest person I've ever met. The way you leapt in front of Ragewing..." The spot between his eyebrows wrinkled and he shook his head slightly, his gaze going wistful. "The youngling alone could have ended you before you could shout *I'm an idiot.*"

"I know that."

"Do you?"

"Yes. I've seen riders scorched to ash during the bonding period. I lost two friends at Grimsbrook and I wasn't even—" Tahlia stopped herself. She'd almost told him the truth about not being there for very long. "I have seen the dark side of riding dragons. But what kind of Mist Knight would I be if I didn't risk my life to save a youngling? There are so few! Have you read up on the latest report of breeding in the wilderness beyond Sunthrone?"

"I..."

"It's terrible. We must make younglings and breeding a priority. There are worse ways to die than for a cause one believes in."

Tilting his head, he studied her, and his gaze was like a touch on her cheeks, her forehead... He wasn't meeting her eyes. Quickly, he began studying the parchment he'd been reading when she'd walked up.

"You are in. For now," he said without glancing her way. "I will send a Leatherworker to you for a fitting immediately. Meet her in your chamber. The guards will know where to find you. Dismissed."

Tahlia stared, her body frozen. She was in. She was allowed to compete for a place in the Mist Knights. This was no dream. It was real. True. Mentally stirring herself to action, she grabbed his hand to shake it.

"Thank you, sir..." The feel of his warm, calloused hand on hers sent heat simmering up her arm. Blinking, she licked her lips. His gaze snagged on her mouth and remained. "I mean, High Captain. Thank you! You won't regret this decision."

She released his hand and slid out of the chair.

Without a backward look, she strode into the tavern crowd to seek out Fara. They had to get back to the chamber for the fitting and for sleep. Tomorrow, it all began.

"I was born to ride dragons," she whispered to herself, "and no one can steal my fate."

CHAPTER 9
MARIUS

Marius raised a hand and one of the Brass Lantern's barkeeps came running.

"Sir, how can I help?"

"Will you have one of your trusted fellows to take this message to the Leatherworker at the end of Rumbling Lane?" He handed over a note he'd written about Tahlia and her needs with regard to new riding leathers. He'd promised a king's sum for a quick job overnight. It wouldn't be more than the male had managed before for Marius.

Finishing the ale he'd ordered after Tahlia's exit, Marius gathered his materials and set off for the commander's chambers. Tahlia's fierce defense of her actions in the arena rang through his head despite his best efforts to stop thinking about her.

THE COMMANDER'S palatial chambers spread across the very top floor of the Mist Knight's castle. A platform operated by staff who worked an elaborate pulley system deposited Marius at the door rather quickly. A servant let him in and Marius awaited the commander and Ophelia for an evening drink they had arranged earlier. The foyer of the lodgings was set with crystalline floors in a mosaic pattern, and the windows looked over the cliffs to distant peaks ringed in fog and ripe valleys illuminated by the moon and stars. The commander's chambers brought truth to what the newcomers called the Mist Knights' castle—the castle in the sky.

But even all the beauty couldn't calm his nerves.

Tonight, he would ask for Ophelia's hand in marriage.

It begins now, Bellona. I will make you proud. Your sacrifice will not be wasted.

His chest ached still for his long-dead sister. He would forget the loss for a day or so, and then, just when he least expected it, the grief hit him like a trebuchet's stone.

"Ah, Marius, so good to see you." Commander Gaius walked into the room. He had slicked his blue-green hair—the same shade as his daughter's—away from his face and his gaze was as cool as it ever was. This male was always very in control of his feelings and he never let anyone see more than he wanted them to see.

Marius stood from the pillowed stool he'd been provided and bowed curtly. "Commander Gaius. I hope this evening finds you well."

"Ophelia says you have something to ask me. She will be here shortly. Her new valet required a bit of a talk."

Marius honestly didn't want to know why Ophelia had yet another new valet.

"Yes, should we wait for her?"

"Of course." Gaius called for crystal wine and had Marius join him in sitting by the snapping fire at the far end of the room.

The wine was exquisite, just like the commander's clothing and chambers. All was in its proper place and in the best condition. Gaius did everything the way Marius endeavored to do. If Marius played his cards right, he would be just like Gaius someday. Marius's father, Aloysius, had been a good male, but not the type one looks up to. He'd been messy and forgetful. And he'd made one terrible mistake after another. In low moments, Marius believed Aloysius had brought death upon himself and upon Marius's mother as well. If he'd been paying more attention to detail, Aloysius and Marius's mother wouldn't have been visiting a fever-stricken town.

Gaius sipped his wine from a rare Murrina cup. The carver's resin applied to the purple, green, and pink fluorite was known to give the contents a unique flavor. "How did your interviews go?"

Stomach tightening with nerves, Marius drank most of the wine from the Murrina cup Gaius had given him. "Good. I only sent one away. An older male who didn't have the experience necessary."

Nodding, Gaius motioned for the servant to pour more wine for Marius. "How many competitors do we have this year?"

"Eleven."

"Have any bets on who will win the position?"

"Not yet. I've only seen those I interviewed."

"You didn't eat with the others?"

Mealtimes with his fellow knights provided not

just food, but information on the goings-on. "No, I was early to the Brass Lantern and ate there."

Ophelia strode into the room wearing a heavily embroidered dress and her golden laurels. "I hope I didn't keep you waiting long."

Her gaze found Marius's and she raised an eyebrow and parted her lips. She was a handsome woman and many suitors had knocked on her chamber door over the last two years, but thus far, she had only paid attention to Marius. He was proud of that fact, but he wished his body stirred when she came near. Surely, at some point he would find her physically attractive.

He stood and kissed her cheek. She smelled of the thyme honey lotion she used daily. Gaius handed her a cup of wine from the servant's tray. She sipped and joined them by the fire.

"What have you two been discussing? The interviews, I'd guess?"

"Yes," her father answered. "We only lost one in the process."

"Odd that we only had twelve attempt to compete. Everyone is scared of our High Captain." She nudged Marius with an elbow. "Don't you ever stop being your vicious self, darling."

Gaius eyed Marius. "I don't think we need to

worry about that. Marius is as predictable as the sunset."

"Unless he is in the air." Ophelia's eyes went hazy, her attraction to Marius obvious.

Marius realized he was frowning. He worked his features into a less severe countenance. "I think it's the weather more than anything. Those late snows kept some from travel." It was springtime in the mountains now, but the realm was large and travel wasn't easy for everyone even when they were only a mountain or two away.

"He's too humble, our High Captain is," Gaius said, raising his cup to Ophelia.

She raised hers too.

Marius grumbled and finished his wine. He'd grown up on watered crystal wine, so it didn't hit him like it did newcomers. He'd forgotten to warn the interviewees about that particular danger... He would need to send messages out tonight before anyone ended up completely hammered from the special drink.

"So, Marius." Gaius leaned forward and rested his elbows on his knees. The edges of his eyes showed his years. "You had something to ask me?"

His stomach twisted. Would Gaius say yes or have him thrown out?

"I have come to ask for Ophelia's hand in marriage."

Gaius smiled warmly. Ah, he'd already known. Of course he had. The male knew everything that happened or was even about to happen on the mountain.

Standing, Gaius raised his cup. "I give my blessing to what will become the most powerful couple in any realm!"

Ophelia kissed Marius fully on the lips, and he pulled away, not wishing to display so much affection in front of her father. A scowl shadowed her face for a second, but soon she was smiling again.

"Thank you, Father. I agree. We are going to rule this mountain."

Her eyes glittered like a snake's and Marius's stomach knotted. Was he making a mistake? Surely not. He mentally shook off the worry and raised his cup, toasting to Gaius's good health and Ophelia's prowess in the sky.

Gaius excused himself to talk to a servant, leaving Ophelia with Marius.

What would Ophelia have done in Tahlia's place when the youngling ran free? Ophelia smoothed her gold-threaded dress and sat beside Marius. No, she wouldn't have risked her life for the dragons. Unless glory would have come from the action. But that was wise; that was basically what he'd told Tahlia—that her actions had been foolish. Why could he not stop wondering and thinking about her?

"What's wrong, darling?" Ophelia touched his shoulder as a servant approached Gaius and asked about instructions for tomorrow's event.

"Nothing. Thank you. I'm simply tired. I might go soon. Would that disappoint you?"

"I'd rather you stay for a while. We should burn a dragon lavender to commemorate our engagement."

Something about talking to Ophelia now felt hollow when compared to his tension-filled interview with Tahlia. He studied Ophelia's face and the look she wore when glancing over at her father. Who was she really? He had never asked her many personal questions about courage and why she rode dragons. How could he wed someone simply based on their blood?

"Yes. Let's do that," he said finally.

He walked with her to the small garden that grew outside the balcony doors. The moonlight scattered over the dragon lavender's dark purple blooms and patterned leaves. The lines in the leaves resembled dragon scales. Together, they plucked a leaf and a bloom each and started back inside.

Marius stopped Ophelia with a hand to her arm. "Can I ask you something as your intended, not as your High Captain?"

"Anything."

"Why do you ride?"

"It was my destiny to ride dragons. Could I have been anything else with a father like mine?"

He lifted his eyebrows and watched Gaius through the uneven glass of the balcony window. "Probably not. But really, what do you love about it?"

Ophelia's lips bunched and she looked out over the cliffs. "I can't say I love it any more than other exciting pastimes like dancing, gambling, or even dazzling my intended with seduction." She faced him and ran a hand down his torso, then along the inner side of his thigh. Her lips found the crook of his neck and she kissed him there. The scent of her lotion made his head pound.

She drew back and eyed him warily. "Don't you like me touching you?"

"I do. Of course I do."

She crossed her arms. "You'll have to do better

than that to persuade me to spend all my years in your bed."

He forced a chuckle, his stomach turning. Why didn't his body respond to her? She was beautiful. Strong. Smart. He wanted her. Leaning close, he swept his hands up to her face and cradled her jaw. The lavender wedged between his fingers touched her ear.

"How is this?" He set his mouth to hers and slowly licked her upper lip.

She moaned and pressed against him. "Let's go to my chamber."

"Your father is here. I'd rather wait until...a better time." He stepped back, wishing his heart had been beating as quickly as Ophelia's.

Her lips became a flat line, but she nodded. "I understand. I was just carried away." A rare smile softened her face.

Was he being silly? They were adults. They were engaged. But it felt wrong to be so emotional in front of the commander even if he did approve of their relationship.

THEY WENT BACK INSIDE and joined Gaius. At the commander's crystal altar, Marius and Ophelia placed their dragon lavender into the rose-hued bowl and Gaius lit the offerings. As the sweet and smoky scent laced the air, Marius started to speak the ritual words, but Gaius beat him to it.

"Bless these two in their coming union and in the joining of two great minds and hearts. May their lives be long and fruitful, filled with the rage of dragons and the defeat of their enemies."

Marius and Ophelia knelt for a moment, then stood up again. They set their fists to their right temple each, a sign of understanding and the final step in this small ritual.

After another glass of wine by the fire, a heated discussion arose about the competitors.

"The Bloodworkers have four samples with significantly high amounts of Mistgold," Gaius said. "We should pull from that small group instead of keeping it open to lesser bloods."

Ophelia stared at the fire and ran her finger over the edge of her cup. "I agree."

"But why not test all those who passed the first steps?" Marius asked. "The ones with the best blood might be terrible on dragonback."

Gaius brushed some lavender ash from his sleeve. "But their training is noted, and with that much Mist Fae blood, they wouldn't have been able to lie."

Marius moved his cup from hand to hand and back again. Why had he even said that to Gaius? All the best dragon riders had extremely high levels of Mistgold in their veins.

"True," Marius said. "Do you want to change the tournament process now? For tomorrow?" It was too fast, but if Gaius demanded the change... That would be chaotic at best and terms for a small revolt if things went south.

"No, not for this one. But next time, I think you should see to that."

"Me?"

"Once you are wed to Ophelia and your life is settled, I'm going to step down and suggest you as my replacement."

Marius gripped the cup so hard that his forefinger knuckle popped. This was what he'd always wanted. So why was his head pounding and his stomach twisting? Perhaps he was afraid of failure.

"Thank you very much, Commander. I'm flattered."

"It's not flattery. You lead better than I ever did and you're an ace in the air. I want only the best for you," he said, turning to face Ophelia, "and this male is the best."

Ophelia tilted her head and regarded her father. "Are you certain you're ready to step down?"

"I'm ready as soon as you are."

As soon as Marius and Ophelia were ready to wed, he meant. This was good. So good. Wasn't it? They would marry very soon and Marius would become commander.

Marius stood. "I'm afraid I have a headache. I need some rest. We can set a date for the wedding after the tournament. Does that work for you?"

He examined his future wife's features, wishing she had truly answered his earlier question about dragon riding.

"I say we wed exactly one week from today."

"So soon?" Marius's palms grew damp. "Why rush? We can plan a proper feast and gathering if we have more time."

Gaius rubbed his chin and glanced from Ophelia to Marius. "No reason to wait for a party you wouldn't even wish to attend, Marius."

It was true. Marius was not the festival type. He much preferred a book and an early bedtime—so much the better for early morning riding and training.

"No," the commander continued, "the wedding will be held in one week. Prepare as you see fit and I will call in my steward to handle the larger details."

"All right." Marius bowed to each of them and left quickly.

He would be married this time next week. Shaking his head, he rapped the outer door to call up the moving platform. The pulley squeaked quietly and soon Marius was back in his room, lying on his bed and wondering at the untamable storm inside his heart.

CHAPTER 10

TAHLIA

"Are you sure I don't look fully ridiculous?" Tahlia examined her reflection in the mirror. The new leather armor had arrived before sunup. "I had no idea they would fit so much more tightly in the legs."

Fara lay on her bed, one arm slung over her forehead. "And they work so much better with your up top assets. You look amazing."

"I look naked."

"It's just that you have more curves than most riders. These fine leathers were literally made for your shape."

"I feel a bit exposed though." Tahlia turned and grimaced at her arse in the reflection. It wasn't that she didn't like her body, but she'd never worn anything so revealing in the way it fit every line and angle of her body. It was making her uncharacteristically shy.

Sitting up and rubbing her temples, Fara let out a groan. "Why did you let me drink that terrifying crystal wine? I forgot how strong they make it for the Mist Fae."

"I wasn't even around when you were enthusiastically imbibing."

Fara spread her purple arms wide. "I was just worried about your interview."

"You didn't need to worry. I told you. It went well...I think." Tahlia knew she could be overly optimistic. Was she wrong? No, he had approved her admission to the tournament and he had sent her this armor.

"Well, now *I'm* telling *you* to stop fretting for once," Fara said. "The Leatherworker assured me this was proper and ordered by the High Captain himself."

Tahlia pulled at the bottom of the vest. The armor was actually incredibly comfortable, far less stiff than the set she'd used to gain entrance to the mountain as a potential competitor. But she felt like her body was being exposed as sensual rather than tough.

"I can be attractive and tough, right? Even though I'm shorter than I'd like?"

"You definitely are. Attractive and tough, I mean, not short. But you *are* that too. Stop fussing. You look astoundingly glorious, like a war goddess come down to the mountain."

Tahlia laughed. "Thanks, friend."

"You're going to drop jaws and then you'll awe them with your riding skills. If they don't find out about your blood and put you to death by dragon fire."

"You were doing so well there for a moment."

Fara collapsed back on the bed and shut her eyes. "I hate to tell you this, but you're going to have to attend the Presentation of the Competitors without me. Unless you like a whining vomiter at your back."

Tahlia dampened a washing cloth in the basin sitting on the small table between their beds, set it on her friend's forehead, and let it fall over her eyes. Fara let out a sigh of relief.

"You sure?"

"Am I sure I don't want to heave last night's dinner all over your fancy new outfit? Yes, I'm quite positive about that. You won't fire me for this, will you, boss?"

Tahlia chuckled. "It's only your first offense. I'll allow at least two mistakes."

"Gee, you are kind." Fara smacked her leg lightly. "Now, go. Or you'll be late and they might not let you into the hall. I heard the king and queen were already seated and taking supplicants' questions."

"Heal up quickly. I'll need you in an hour. I can't go out there alone."

"You could, but you won't have to." Fara moved the cloth to wink.

With a deep breath, Tahlia nodded and stood. She picked up her new helmet with its red plumage.

It was tournament time.

LIGHT from the long windows sparkled across the dragon-sized crystals that adorned the great hall's ceiling and walls. Rosy pink, ocean-toned blue, and deep indigo spread over the gathering crowd of Mist Knights in their pale leathers and red-tufted helmets, velvet-wrapped nobles of the Shrouded Mountains region talking animatedly, and a good number of common folk in homespun wool looking on with wide eyes.

Holding her helmet under her arm, Tahlia took a

spot near the front of the crowd, beside the other Mist Knights and competitors, with the nobles to their right and the common folk to the left of the room.

On the dais, Seelie King Lysanael, and his mate, Queen Revna of Isernwyrd, sat on tall black-stained wooden thrones. Beside Queen Revna, a shadow materialized and became a forest dragon. Like all forest dragons, he was much smaller than mountain dragons and the power of invisibility ran through his veins. The dragon—Arkyn, Tahlia thought she'd heard him called—currently had his snout in a large copper bowl of something that was staining his snout a dark blue.

Beside Arkyn, a man in a helmet with blue tuffs rather than red stood stiffly, the ends of his blue-green hair showing. Commander Gaius. He honestly scared Tahlia more than any dragon could. Hands clasped, he leaned toward the king and queen. King Lysanael's dark crown glittered atop his head of obsidian-dark hair as he nodded at something the commander had said. Queen Revna eyed the crowd like she was measuring each person up for a fight. Her hand went to her dragon and she slid her palm down his neck. Arkyn shuffled his wings and settled himself on the ground beside the queen with his tail extended behind the commander. It reached all the way to the steps on the side where two more Mist Knights approached. Ah, it was Marius and that foul, high-ranking female from the baths. Marius held his helmet and searched the room with his stormy eyes.

His gaze stopped on Tahlia. He tripped and swore loudly, glancing backward at Arkyn's tail, which was slapping the dais like a happy dog's might. Was Marius all right? Maybe he was hungover like Fara. Marius looked up and his focus locked onto Tahlia. A flush darkened his cheeks and she bit her lip to keep from chuckling.

He spoke in the female's ear and she turned a glare on Tahlia. What were they saying? Had they found out about the feigned blood sample?

CHAPTER 11
MARIUS

Marius cleared his throat, straightened, then bowed to the king and queen with as much dignity as he could manage after tripping over a dragon. Ophelia curtseyed alongside him.

Queen Revna smirked. "A legendary dragon rider who trips over the beast's tail? There must be something truly interesting in the crowd to have distracted one as experienced as you, High Captain."

Only recently had the royals been taking part in festivities on the mountain. Marius wished they'd never come.

Gaius's intense stare was practically scorching Marius's cheek. Marius did his best to act as though nothing was amiss and the mere sight of Tahlia's arresting curves hadn't swept his feet right out from under him. There had been a dragon tail involved, but he never would have tripped so easily had it not been for the shock of desire that had hit him upon seeing Tahlia.

"I didn't sleep as much as I would have liked, Your Majesty," Marius said to the queen. It was true and tasted so on his tongue, but it wasn't the whole truth.

The queen raised an eyebrow. Her eyes were so odd, completely human and icy pale. "Right."

King Lysanael smiled at his wife, then his eyes drew downward and he pursed his lips. "I'd like to mention my fallen brother as we open. Would that break any cultural norms, Commander Gaius?"

"Mist Knights always honor our fallen," the commander said, bowing slightly. "Please, feel free to express your respect for your loved one."

King Lysanael rose from his temporary throne and extended a hand to his queen, who took it and stood with him. "Greetings, knights, nobles, and folk of the mountains."

The crowd bowed and curtseyed, their gazes locked on the dais as they studied the king and queen, the commander, Marius, and Ophelia.

"What is wrong with you?" Ophelia hissed.

"I tripped."

"I noticed, but you seem flustered."

Ophelia's glance went from his face to the crowd.

Marius didn't want to know if she saw Tahlia and could read anything from the way he had looked at the competitor. He focused his gaze on the back wall.

King Lysanael was recounting the history of the older brother he'd lost to the weather here in the Shrouded Mountains. "All he wanted was to be one of the knights of legend, to ride into the clouds to glory." The king bowed his head and his chest moved in a deep, slow breath. Queen Revna took his hand in hers. He smiled at her, then regarded the crowd once more. "I honor him by attending this year's tournament. In his name, I will give the next Mist Knight named a parcel of land near my winery, a place dear to my heart."

The crowd let out a cheer of excitement.

The king raised a hand to quiet them. "Now, I believe it's time for the Presentation of Competitors!"

Another shout of joy went up and filled the great hall with noise. Marius wished this pageantry was over because the sooner they flew with the competitors, the better. The breeze this morning smelled of a storm.

Gaius went to the other end of the dais and called up the competitors as the king and queen took their seats.

"Lord Renwall of Turnlington," the commander called out.

Renwall stalked up the steps to Marius, who was required to kiss both the male's cheeks in a ridiculous old tradition.

"What is the deal with the kissing?" the queen whispered as Renwall walked away from the dais.

Ophelia gave the queen a polite smile. "At the very first tournament, the High Captain of that time kissed his lead rider for luck. The rider ended up abed with a fever while the rest went flying to drive back pirates coming inland up north. All of the dragons and their riders died that day except for the one who had been ill. That's why the High Captain's kiss is known to be good luck. It's an odd tradition, granted. But we are used to it."

Queen Revna shrugged. "I'm all for more kissing." She winked at Marius, then cut her eyes in the direction of the crowd.

He knew where she was looking and forced

himself not to follow her gaze to Tahlia. Ophelia would notice and there would be more questions.

Marius twisted slightly to look at Arkyn, Her Majesty's dragon. "Is your dragon feeling under the weather?" He mentioned the dragon to get the queen's focus off of him, but Arkyn did seem a bit lethargic.

The queen snorted. "He ate too many of those fine blueberries your staff provided."

Gaius called out another competitor.

"Serves you right, little monster," the queen whispered to the dragon.

Well, she wasn't the queen he had expected. Far too relaxed for a public appearance.

Marius kept kissing competitors until the moment he had been dreading arose.

"Lady Tahlia of Northwoods."

He stared at the back wall like it held the answer to every mystery in life.

And then she was standing in front of him. In those body-hugging leathers. With that pouty mouth of hers.

He swallowed, looked at her perpetually smiling face, and shifted to the left to kiss the first cheek.

"Thanks again for the armor," she whispered.

Stiffening, he leaned right to finish the job. She

needed to keep that to herself. If Ophelia heard that... Her father probably already knew about the kindness he'd shown Tahlia, but it wasn't all bad. They had helped out competitors with lighter purses in past tournaments. But Ophelia would have serious questions if she found out.

"I said *thank you*."

He grunted. Tahlia's scent enveloped him—something like lemon and spring leaves—and he kissed her second cheek. Her skin was so soft. She said another couple of words, but his heart was beating and he was so worried that he didn't hear any of it. She was gone from the dais in what felt like both the shortest and somehow the longest moment of his life thus far. Well, perhaps not as long as that one day in battle with the pirates, but still...

He forced himself not to watch Tahlia leave the dais as Gaius called another competitor's name.

"Marius." Ophelia's voice was a whisper. "What was she thanking you for?"

"I interviewed her." Not a lie...

"So it went well."

He clenched his jaw. "She knows more about dragons than I did when I first competed for my place."

Ophelia nodded.

"She is reckless, but I'm hoping it isn't a constant with her," he said, tightly.

"None of it matters if she can't fly or fight better than the rest."

"True."

His gaze disobediently strayed to where Tahlia now stood with the knights, their families, and their staff. Maybe she would fail the first trial and his life would go back to normal. He took a deep breath and forced his focus back to King Lysanael and Queen Revna, who had stood.

"Thank you for welcoming us so kindly," the king said to the crowd. "We look forward to a day of what you do best—dragon riding!"

A cheer rang through the hall and though a few of the competitors wore wide smiles, a couple looked ready to spill their breakfast onto the ground. He wouldn't look at Tahlia, but he could guess she was one of the smiling ones.

"Are you thinking about our engagement announcement?" Ophelia eyed him, a bit of what seemed like genuine joy in her eyes.

"When should we tell everyone?" he asked, carefully avoiding her direct question.

The presentation was over and the knights,

commoners, and nobles began to disperse, heading out the main doors.

"At the announcement of the winner maybe?"

He nodded and imagined his life as a checklist. He had gained the rank of High Captain. Helped the order grow stronger. Bonded with a dragon successfully. And now he had the promise of the commander's daughter's hand in marriage. Everything was progressing according to his long-term plan.

Ophelia took Marius's arm and they followed the crowd. Excited conversations were broken by the occasional roar of a dragon. Earlier, the squires had assembled the mounts in the arena. Onlookers could enjoy the sight as the first trial—ground weapons—started.

Inside the now packed and chaotic arena, Marius gave Ophelia's hand a kiss and they broke away, each heading to their judging position on opposite sides of the two rings set up at the northern end of the arena. Competitors and their squires practiced in dirt tracks along the sides of the public seating. Nobles and the common folk filled the public seating on the raised sets of benches arranged on both sides of the tournament grounds. King Lysanael, Queen Revna, Arkyn the forest dragon, and Gaius climbed into the royal box to watch the proceedings.

The first knight to arrive in Marius's ring was, of course, Tahlia with her short gladius sword in hand. Palms sweating, he swallowed and maintained an emotionless expression that was proper for judging.

"Hello again!" She waved like children did, so enthusiastic and witless.

This was a deadly tournament and a serious possible appointment to the Fae military. She needed to stop acting so damn happy. It was going to get her killed.

Her opponent entered the ring. Twice her size, muscled like an ox, and wearing well-oiled and tidy armor, this male was the perfect competitor. A likely winner. The male showed calm, attention to detail, and the correct level of sober attitude. Good. Tahlia would lose immediately, and it would be the beginning of the end for her here on the mountain. He should never have helped her with new armor or passed her through the interview. He couldn't wait for her to be gone.

CHAPTER 12

TAHLIA

The giant male's sword crashed toward Tahlia's head. But where she'd thought maybe he'd be a bit lumbering due to his impressive size, he was sadly quite quick. She lunged sideways and a lock of her hair fell to the sandy earth.

"Thanks for that," she said, panting. "It was getting in my eyes. I thought we were supposed to be using the flat of our blades." She glanced at Marius. "High Captain, isn't that the rule here?"

She spun and thrust her gladius toward the giant male's kidney, turning the sword so it would just smack him and not pierce the leather vest.

"Flats, yes," Marius said, his arms crossed and his stormy gaze locked on her opponent.

Though he agreed, he didn't seem overly concerned with the giant male nearly slicing her in two.

They fought on, her going low mostly and him high. Once she had him lulled into a rhythm, she threw her blade at his chest, timing it so it would hit hilt first. The hilt bumped the male and he stumbled back a step.

Marius cocked his head, then looked toward the three scribes jotting down points. "Death hit. Lady Tahlia of Northwoods is the winner."

The scribes agreed, and Tahlia was announced as moving on to the next round. Fara jogged up and handed Tahlia a small bucket and a ladle. Tahlia tucked her gladius into its sheath and scooped a serving of mint-scented water. It tasted divine.

"Thanks, squire."

"Of course, my lady."

"You still look green around the gills."

"I feel like death, but I'm not going to fail you."

Tahlia returned the small bucket. "You're the best squire in the world, Fara."

"I'm really not."

"You put mint in my water." Tahlia exhaled, enjoying the fresh feel on her tongue. "That's fabulous."

"No, I didn't."

"But it smells like mint," Tahlia said.

Marius lunged forward and grabbed her arm. "What did you say?"

"I said it smells minty. How is that bad?"

Swallowing, Marius held her in place. He shouted a question, but he sounded like he was underwater.

"What did you say?" The arena began to spin. "I can't hear you."

Tahlia rubbed her face with numb hands.

"Tahlia?" Fara's voice was pitched too high.

What was happening?

"Sit down, competitor," Marius said. At least that's what it sounded like.

"I don't feel quite right."

The arena tilted sideways and night fell.

TAHLIA WOKE in Marius's arms. Very strong arms. His hand cradled her head as she blinked and dots swam in front of her eyes. What was happening? He was shouting at someone.

"...and I said immediately and don't bother with Felix. Only bring me Albus! I swear, if you don't get back here in one minute, I will—" His warning broke off as he looked down at her. "You're awake. Thank the Old Ones." His thumb stroked the top edge of her cheek and part of her ear. "Can you hear me? Sometimes ghostmint steals your hearing for a day."

"I can hear you." Her throat felt like it was made of sand.

His eyes pressed shut, then he opened them again to study her face and body. "Does your stomach cramp?"

"No, I just feel... I'm a little beat up but that's probably more from the giant sword-wielder than from... What happened? What is ghostmint?"

The scrabbling sound of feet on the ground and the raging torrent of Fara cursing like a pirate covered whatever Marius tried to say in answer. Tahlia attempted to sit up, but the arena spun and Marius urged her back down.

"Who is Fara destroying?"

"She tried to take Remus's arms."

"Who is Remus?"

"He is my squire and not guilty of this crime. Someone poisoned you and we have yet to find out who. I guess the why is the favor I showed you by gifting you those leathers. Yes, the Leatherworker didn't keep his tongue and now all know that I did you a kindness."

"Another competitor wanted me out of the tournament?"

"Yes, so they poisoned you. Or had someone else do the deed. We will find the culprit and I will see them weep on their knees before you."

"Fara is just trying to annihilate Remus because she needs to murder someone."

"Seems so."

"That's her typical response. Attack and ask questions later."

"So when you say you've been around dragons for a long time..." He studied Fara.

Tahlia chuckled and pain lanced through her throat.

"Just be still," Marius said. "Our best healer is on his way. He has a tonic that will help."

"I won the first bout."

"Yes, and you lived through a poisoning."

"I didn't miss my second match, did I?"

"No, I called a stop to the tournament for the moment."

A male with deep wrinkles and a nose like a crow's beak hustled over and knelt. He pulled a vial from his cloak and gave it to Marius. "Drink that,

Lady Tahlia. It will drive the rest of the poison from your pores and set you to rights. You did quite well considering you smelled the ghostmint before drinking. The High Captain told the messenger that you could scent the mint odor."

"What do you mean?" Tahlia imbibed the bitter contents of the vial. The fluid made her lips pucker but cooled her throat nicely.

"I am Healer Albus. I have had experience with ghostmint plenty of times. The herb possesses a very subtle scent. There had to be a rather daunting dose in your water bucket for you to smell it."

A thought about the poison touched Tahlia's mind, then slipped away before she could actually pay attention to it. Hmm...

"Now," Albus said taking her forearm firmly, "hold still."

He flashed something small and gold across her skin and she felt as if she had been bitten.

"What was that?" she asked.

Albus and Marius traded a look full of narrowed eyes and male know-it-all-ness.

Marius helped Albus smear a dab of something sticky over her forearm. "Albus is just taking care of you. Don't worry."

"I'll test it to be sure the dose isn't hiding," Albus said quietly.

Marius raised both eyebrows. "Like it did with Honorus?"

They whispered on, and Tahlia shook her head to try to hear better. Her vision cleared further and she moved her jaw to pop her ears. The strange feeling the ghostmint had caused passed.

"Can I get up now?" Tahlia asked. "I feel all right."

Fara broke from the two squires who had been holding her away from Remus and his blackened eye. She ran to Tahlia and practically snarled at Marius.

"What happened? Do you know what happened to her?"

"A poison." Tahlia really needed Fara to stop shouting at the High Captain in such an accusatory tone. "But I'm fine."

Albus nodded. "She is remarkably strong, this one."

"My lady is the strongest!" Fara said, taking Tahlia's arm and helping her up.

"Maybe you should rest for a while longer," Marius said.

Tahlia frowned. "I can't hold up the tournament."

The severe female who had snapped at Tahlia in the baths and had stood beside Marius at the presentation walked up. The wind lifted the braided ends of her blue-green hair. "No, you can't. High Captain, it is past time we continue."

"Lady Ophelia, we will resume the tournament when I see fit."

Ophelia's eyebrow twitched and she stared at Tahlia like she was a bug about to be squashed beneath her boot. "The commander says we must begin now."

Was Commander Gaius this female's father? They had the same color hair, so it wouldn't have been surprising.

Marius glanced at the royal box and the commander gave him a quick nod. "Indeed," Marius said with an unreadable look at Tahlia. "Prepare for your next sword fight, competitor."

Everyone but Fara left Tahlia's side of the fighting ring. "You're well enough to do this now?"

"I am," Tahlia said. "I have to be."

Fara handed her sword over. She must have picked it up when Tahlia fell. "Your opponent isn't quite as big this time. That's one small mercy. I swear, when I find out who poisoned you, I'm going to disembowel them right in front of that Ophelia hag."

Tahlia had to laugh. "Calm down. We knew this tournament would be dangerous. I survived and now I'll be extra careful about what I take in and who is around."

Chest puffing in a deep inhale, Fara shook her head. "I wish you had more time to recover."

Tahlia clapped a hand on Fara's shoulder. "I'm fine." She lifted her gladius and faced her second opponent.

Her vision was still foggy, but she could see well enough to fight and her muscles were moving like normal.

The male across the ring from her also fought with a shorter sword and his grin said he knew very well how to use it.

Tahlia widened her stance and waited for him to attack.

CHAPTER 13

MARIUS

Marius finished reporting to Gaius, who had wanted every detail about what happened to Tahlia.

"Thank you, High Captain." Gaius sat back in his chair beside the king and queen. "You should return to your judging because I don't trust Sir Titus as much as I do you."

King Lysanael leaned on the arm of his chair. His gaze scanned the arena as the competitors continued their ground-fighting trials. "Who do you believe is responsible for the poisoning?"

"We have no leads on that as of yet," Marius said.

Queen Revna scratched the underside of her dragon's chin. Ten seats had been removed from the public seating to allow for Arkyn's size. "I've never heard of ghostmint."

"It can be used for healing if given in the right doses," Marius said. "The herb is common in these altitudes."

"I'll have to get a sample of that," the queen said, her icy eyes glittering with fascination.

Marius remembered she used to be an assassin for the human king. "I will see to it, Your Majesty."

He bowed and returned to the arena. Tahlia was clearly winning, her opponent sweating like a fevered dog and kneeling on the sandy ground. Titus called the result, and after two more rounds that ended in a similar fashion, the ground trials were over and the scribes were tallying points.

Tahlia was in the top five, and Marius wasn't getting his wish that she would be leaving the mountain.

Marius led the competitors to the dragons assembled at the other end of the arena. "Now you will meet each dragon and they will choose one of you for the next trial."

ALISHA KLAPHEKE

"They choose?" A male missing an ear looked at the mounts with wide eyes.

Marius grunted. "Do they not choose their riders at Grimsbrook?"

All of the competitors had trained at one of the dragon riding schools around the realm. Most had the same policies, but differences did arise here and there.

"They used to." Tahlia's voice was brighter than it should have been after her terrifying day. "But they are running low on dragons, from what I heard."

"It is a concern, certainly," Marius said. "Now, walk past the dragons in a slow and steady line. Allow them to scent you. You will know when you have been accepted or rejected."

The competitors did as ordered. The male first in line ducked as a Seabreak lashed its head at him. A rejection. He strode past a Heartsworn and two Spikebacks who acted like he wasn't even there. Finally, a juvenile Green-flanked Terror lowered his head to the male.

"The Terror has chosen you," Marius explained. "We can only set new riders on a Terror when they are young. You must remember this dragon doesn't have much rider experience at all and he may dive too quickly during exercises. Keep him in check. If you are capable of doing so. If not, well, you might not last the day."

The male paled slightly but grabbed the Terror's reins and led him toward the spot where everyone would takeoff for the flying trial.

More dragons chose more riders and finally it was Tahlia's turn. The Spikebacks growled in unison as she passed them. Interesting. What didn't they like about her? Perhaps she still smelled of ghost-mint. Dragons loathed the odor of that herb. She came to a stop at the one Seabreak and looked up at the dragon's ocean-blue head, seemingly unafraid. The dragon lifted its snout and roared, causing a few youngling Fae watching past the fence to scatter.

Tahlia set her hands on her hips. "Come on, gorgeous, I know it's you."

"How do you know?" Marius asked.

"I've always had an affinity to water. Plus, she feels...right."

"That's either incredibly powerful intuition you have, competitor, or you are simply good at pretend-ing. I hope it's the first or she might strike you down."

"She won't."

Tahlia stepped closer to the Seabreak and the

dragon flapped its set of four wings. The shell-shaped, pearly-white stripes along its neck and sides caught the sun and made Marius blink. She was a beautiful dragon.

The Seabreak sniffed Tahlia's head, then set its snout against her stomach. Tahlia turned, grinning from ear to ear. "See? We are meant for one another!"

"For today's trials only. You can't bond unless you win this tournament. She will get over you when you leave. Don't think she is as loyal as the dragons in the old tales. Bonds like that take years to form and solidify."

Tahlia rubbed the Seabreak's neck and cooed at the creature. "Grouchy High Captain thinks you don't really like me, but we know the truth, don't we?"

Marius rolled his eyes. He waved at the squires and stable lads standing nearby, then left for the takeoff point.

Remus led Ragewing from the far end of the arena to the point to meet him. Tahlia's ridiculous conversation with the Seabreak continued behind him.

"Do not attempt to name that dragon, Tahlia."

He stopped and looked at the ground.

"You mean Lady Tahlia?" she said, her tone joking.

Damn. He hadn't meant to use her first name without a title. Why did she throw him off so much? Stones, he wished she would just give up this tournament and leave him in peace.

He hurried to Ragewing and mounted up. "Quickly, competitors." He gave each of their dragons a number, one through seven—all that were left of the competitors after the ground trial.

The other Mist Knights stood at attention near their dragons, present for the pageantry. They didn't ride in the flying trial. It was all competitors with Marius giving the commands in the air.

Once all the tournament participants were seated on their dragons, Marius waved for them to launch. Ragewing joined the group, spreading his wings and shooting into the darkening sky.

The sword-like perfume of a coming storm rolled through the churning clouds. The dragons cut through the tattered ends of those clouds. They would have to fly low at first so Marius could judge the riders.

Someone let out a whoop and zipped past. Tahlia. Of course. Her eyes shone with joy and she wasn't even holding on to the reins. He tried to unclench his jaw...

"Slow and in a tight angle formation!" he called out using his powerful voice to be heard over a rumble of thunder.

Would she obey orders or act reckless as she had on the ground?

Tahlia turned her Seabreak and led the rest in forming behind Ragewing and Marius.

"Nice lead, five!"

He could almost feel her smiling. The corners of his mouth twitched and he shook his head. Raising a hand, he led the group on a breathtaking dive. Riding low and close to Ragewing's neck, he turned to glance at Tahlia. She was just a little mound of white and black on the Seabreak's back. Numbers six and four were dragging behind. A point from each of them.

Ragewing responded to Marius's double pat on his scales and pulled up sharply. Tahlia nearly passed him on the right but managed to rein in her dragon and hover in a lovely show of control. She really could ride. Half the others mimicked the movement while the last half were still trying to stop their diving dragons. Number four went into a deadly spin.

Tahlia shouted, but the rising wind stole the words, and then she was launching toward the ground again.

She was going after number four.

"Stop!" he called out.

But Tahlia didn't look back and her dragon kept on. Young dragons sometimes grew so dizzy they couldn't stop spinning until they smashed into the ground. Tahlia urged the Seabreak to fly faster than number four and his Spikeback. Tahlia drove her Seabreak under the other dragon, who shrieked in panic and flipped, halting his downward, deadly spiral. The Spikeback rolled and shook his head while number four held on, pale-faced. Spreading his wings, the Spikeback found his direction and soared upward as his rider regained his position in the saddle.

Tahlia returned to Marius, hair ripped from her braids and her cheeks pink. Number four rose up and joined them and the rest of the competitors, who had finally gathered close to hover.

"Thank you, number five," four called out.

Tahlia waved a quick hand in acknowledgment and looked to Marius. "I apologize for ignoring your command." He could barely hear her.

"If you had failed," he said, "you would be out of

the tournament. Since you saved a rider, you remain. Let us continue." Barking orders, he had the competitors and their mounts fly in tight spirals below the lightning-touched gray clouds. He commanded them to fly in a triangle formation, a double square, and then he ordered them to soar into the storm.

CHAPTER 14
TAHLIA

Lightning cracked the mist, and Tahlia set a hand against the Seabreak, directing the dragon to swoop past the Spikeback that Marius had ordered them to encircle. Only the Spikeback's tail was visible in the churning clouds, but the creature and its rider were hovering, so her spot in the circle wouldn't alter much. The wind rose and howled in her ears and rain lashed through the mist. How was it both misty and pouring? These mountaintop storms were incredible!

"Why are you smiling?" number two, a male competitor on a bright red Heartsworn, called out to her over the wildly beautiful weather.

"Why *aren't* you smiling? This is amazing!"

Tahlia and the Seabreak took up the far spot in the circle of dragons around number three.

Marius's voice boomed in an echo of the thunder. "Well done. Now, drop in a spiral. Number order. Use your instincts to avoid lightning and pay attention to your dragon's natural inclination to avoid being struck as well!"

Fara would die if she knew what I was up to... Tahlia grinned, her heart soaring. The taste of the storm, metallic and green, touched her tongue. Marius looked like one of the Old Ones with his whip curled over his big shoulder and his hair lashing about his chiseled cheekbones and jawline.

His gaze slid to her and his lips parted like he was about to say something.

Looking away quickly, Tahlia focused on her task. Dropping behind number four, she urged the Seabreak to spiral downward. Glimpses of the arena showed between the black and silver clouds—the purple paint of the wooden trim around the walls and the waving arms of the cheering crowd.

Below Tahlia and the Seabreak, competitor two was having trouble. The Heartsworn's wings struggled against the wind. He was holding her reins too tightly.

The tiny hairs on the back of Tahlia's neck stood on end.

"Move!" she shouted.

She turned her dragon left as light washed the world and thunder gripped her ears and ripped into them. Blinking, ears ringing, she held to the Seabreak and whispered words the dragon surely couldn't hear.

"Thank you, love." Tahlia blinked, still trying to see through the spots in her eyes.

The other competitors had scattered with the close strike. Two, seven, nine, and one were gathering themselves into spiral formation again. Tahlia and her Seabreak flew toward them, gaining speed and aiming for their proper position. Others joined in, faces paled—no doubt as pale as hers considering how they had nearly been fried—and soon they had all but one competitor.

Marius and Ragewing were nowhere to be seen in the sky either. Worry pinched at Tahlia's stomach as they flew through another bank of clouds. Surely the High Captain wouldn't have had trouble. She imagined his storm-gray eyes shuttering and his body falling through the clouds. She bit her lip and forced the image out of her mind.

"Where is four?" she called out to the other

competitors. Four was the same rider who had nearly fallen earlier. "Anyone seen the High Captain?"

But Tahlia might as well have been mute for all that she was heard over the lashing rain and rolling thunder. She should have learned the hand signals for communication. They were rarely used because those with strong Mistgold in their blood didn't usually struggle to be heard.

The clouds cleared briefly, and Tahlia looked down to see the arena stretched out below the spiraling dragons.

On the ground, Ragewing stomped impatiently and Marius crouched beside a splayed rider. Next to them, the rider's Spikeback roared in pain and rolled to his side.

But Marius and Ragewing were alive and well. The relief that rolled over Tahlia had her trembling in her saddle. She slicked some wet and fallen hair from her face and readied to land.

The spiral of competitors landed in order, splashing mud everywhere. Tahlia leapt from the Seabreak's back and rushed toward the fallen dragon and rider. Her heart thundered as loudly as the continuing storm. The crowd had gone still and their worry was palpable. The rider's eyes were shut, but his chest moved as Marius spoke over him to Albus, the healer who had helped Tahlia with the poison. Thank the Old Ones, the rider was alive. She turned toward the dragon, who was surrounded by a host of squires and Mist Knights.

"Give him space," Ophelia demanded as she spread a glossy concoction over the blackened scales on the Spikeback's side.

The dragon heaved a deep and shaky breath and his wings shuddered, half open and terribly vulnerable on the muddy ground. One Mist Knight guarded the dragon's head as Ophelia and her squire worked the unguent onto the wounded beast.

"The rider is talking to the High Captain now." Fara's voice was suddenly at Tahlia's shoulder.

"Good."

"They say he was simply knocked out. He wasn't hit like his mount," Fara added.

Tahlia slicked her wet and mussed braids out of her face and looked from rider to dragon and back again. "Poor thing. But dragons handle this sort of thing from time to time."

"Fire, yes, but lightning? Have you heard many stories of them living after a direct hit?"

"I am sure there are cases."

"I hope your optimism is truly on target this

time, friend." Fara put a hand on Tahlia's shoulder and Tahlia gripped Fara's fingers, appreciating the support.

She was shaken, more so than she'd ever been. Not that she would let anyone know, especially Fara, who would likely drag her away from the tournament for fear of her dying.

"You're certain you want to continue?" Fara whispered.

"Completely."

Blowing out a breath, Fara ran her purple hands through her wet hair. "I can't wait until this is over. I just hope I'm not alone at the end of it."

The rider groaned and sat up and the crowd cheered as Marius helped him to standing. The Spikeback huffed and got his legs under him. Ophelia leapt back and the other Mist Knights followed her cue, giving the dragon room. The king, queen, commander, and the onlookers in the stands let out a cry of "Huzzah!"

Tahlia bumped Fara with her shoulder. "You won't be alone. I did well up there."

They hurried to Tahlia's Seabreak, who seemed to be happy, nibbling a bit of greenery that decorated the wall of the arena.

"I want you to do poorly up there," Fara said.

"What?"

Fara held out her hands. "But only so badly that you're kicked out of the lineup, not kicked out of life."

A laugh bubbled from Tahlia amidst the continued cheering. The injured Spikeback was led away and Commander Gaius raised his hands to quiet the masses. Fara helped Tahlia get the Seabreak's reins over her head so Fara could lead her back to the dragon stables.

"We break now for rest and food," the commander said. "The sky battle will commence one bell before sundown. Time is kept on the water clock in the great hall, where all competitors are welcome."

Tahlia shivered with excitement. The sky battle. She had waited her whole life for this.

But first—food. And perhaps a little conversation with the handsome High Captain...

CHAPTER 15
TAHLIA

Loud conversation and the clanking of plates and mugs filled the great hall. The crystals gleamed with magical light overhead—the sage-colored one aided in the dragons' health, the rose-hued crystal encouraged mating when numbers were low, the massive clear crystal formations were said to enable the bonds that formed between dragons and their riders, and the purple and gold ones lent courage to the dragons. They were beautiful, and Tahlia imagined she could feel their benefits even as a non-dragon. She smiled and energy simmered down her back. She always did have a strong imagination. A few Mist Knights, a squire, and a couple of competitors also looked up at the crystals while their neighbors held up mugs in toasts to the day's feats and the coming challenges.

"To number five!" Tahlia's fellow competitors stood and gave her a cheer. Number four remained in the healing wing of the castle keep, but reports said he was well on his way to good health and might even be able to rejoin the tournament.

Tahlia waved at the cheering folk and walked with Fara to a table near the back of the hall, where servants poured in and out with heavy-laden food and drink trays.

Fara inhaled noisily and took a seat beside Tahlia on the bench. "Finally, some real food."

"I don't know if I can eat. I'm too excited."

"But there is cake." Fara raised her eyebrows at a tray a servant was sliding into place at their table.

The cooks and their assistants had set cakes in all the colors of the crystals into ordered concentric circles. Iced images of the dragon subspecies marked the cakes' tops and lacy rings of yet more icing lined the edges of each one.

Fara grabbed two purple and gold ones. "I wonder if these will taste like courage."

Tahlia nabbed a rose-colored one. "What does romance taste like?"

Fara laughed. "Please don't answer that. I'm

afraid of your dirty jokes," she said around a large bite.

The rose cake was soft on the tongue, the perfect type of texture to go with the more sturdy icing. The taste was a blend of white chocolate, rose, and cinnamon. Delicious.

The servants filled their mugs with watered wine, and a piper and a lute-player began a jaunty tune. Three of Tahlia's fellow competitors found an empty area beyond the first set of tables and started to dance.

Fara swirled her mug and sniffed. "There's barely any wine in here at all."

"I suppose they don't fancy the rest of us falling off our dragons."

Glaring, Fara took a drink. She wiped her mouth with a linen napkin and eyed the other people at their table. "Please don't even joke about that."

Tahlia snorted a laugh and enjoyed a white cake that had a pleasant herbal taste to it like a sweet mint with a hint of basil. She washed it down with the watered wine, which somehow complimented the treats in the most lovely way.

The clatter of dice and bones sounded at the table behind them.

"Ah," Fara said dreamily, "the siren song of gambling dice."

Tahlia turned to see Marius engaged in a game with another Mist Knight. The marble gaming board bore a sigil—two lions flanking a dragon's head.

Fara joined Tahlia in staring. "Mist Knights must have even more money than I thought if they have their own marble gaming boards. Look at those carvings."

"I overheard number one saying the knights are given a higher stipend than they previously received due to the increasing threats on the eastern coast." Tahlia wiggled her eyebrows.

Curiosity had Tahlia up and walking over to Marius and his gaming partner. She sat beside the High Captain on the bench. Fara muttered something about "pushing her luck in too many directions," but Tahlia ignored her.

"Is that your board?" she asked Marius.

"It is Titus's." His gaze cut to her then away.

Her heart beat a little faster. He smelled like fire and the stormy air they'd flown in.

"That's a lovely fritillium." She smiled at the wooden dice cup that Titus upturned over the marble board. The surface was a deep rosy hue.

Titus inclined his head. "Made from drag-onwood, of course."

"Of course."

"Want to play?" Titus asked. "I've been rolling dogs. Marius has already beat me soundly. He could use some better competition."

"It's only luck though," Tahlia said.

"Oh, don't tell our High Captain that."

Tahlia looked at the side of Marius's handsome face. "Why? Don't you agree?" His scar caught the light for a moment before he turned toward her.

"If you keep track of the numbers your partner rolls, you can choose which numbers you keep for your count on your rolls," Marius said.

Tahlia winced. "That's a lot of numbers to jam inside your head. Sounds painful."

One of his moon-white eyebrows lifted and he watched her with those stormy eyes of his. Stones, but he was beautiful. And scary. It was a perfect combination. He pursed his full lips and she wondered if they would taste like the drink sitting beside his hand? How would a male like the High Captain kiss? Would he be slow, torturing her with the tip of his tongue as she ached for more? Or would he be aggressive and claim her mouth as his own with a demanding embrace? She cleared her throat and pushed those thoughts away.

"Games are meant to be fun, right?" she asked, frowning at Marius. "They're not supposed to be a lesson in mental tallying."

Titus laughed and covered his mouth with a fist. "Apologies, High Captain. I didn't intend to disrespect you, I—"

Marius waved his apology away. "We are off duty. Relax."

Tahlia snickered and gave Titus a friendly wink. "Oh, really easy to relax with that face of his turning you to stone over the game board, isn't it, Sir Titus?" She froze. Why had she just said that? She decidedly did not look from Titus to Marius. Was she trying to anger him and ruin her chances?

"Your cheeks flush at the slightest thing, don't they?" Marius said.

She slid her gaze to the right. He was studying her face.

Please let the table grow a mouth and eat me whole.

"It's just those stormy eyes of yours," she said quietly, grinning with all of her teeth and hoping to all of the Old Ones that he wouldn't kick her off the mountain right now. "They are just, um, incredibly stern."

Why was she still blabbering? *Shut up, me.* She bit her lip, and Marius's focus narrowed to her mouth. Under his body-clinging leathers, his broad chest shifted in a quick breath.

Titus was shaking, obviously holding in laughter with his pinched lips. Marius eyed her coolly, but though his expression was cold as a Saturnalia morning, she found herself feeling like she'd stumbled into the blazing hearth across the hall.

"I'm not going to eat you alive, Lady Tahlia."

An image of the High Captain setting his sharp teeth against her thigh flashed through her naughty mind. She imagined the feel of his hot tongue on her skin and the slip of his hair through her fingers. Growing far, far too warm between her legs, she coughed and pulled at her undershirt's neckline and prayed for a breeze.

"Of course not," she said nervously. "Let's play, shall we?" She grabbed the dice and bones and tossed them in the fritillium, nearly elbowing Fara, who had appeared suddenly. Tahlia upturned the wooden cup and watched the numbers appear. "Fara!" she said in an overloud and ridiculous tone she couldn't seem to hold back. "Where were you? We were just having a great conversation!"

Fara winced and pulled at her ear. "I was making

you a plate of oysters and venison." She slid the plate toward the gaming board.

"Wonderful! Thank you!"

Tahlia paused in pointing out which numbers she chose to keep as her score and shoved an oyster into her mouth. Spicy heat seared her tongue and ravaged her throat. Sputtering, she managed to get the oyster down.

Marius patted her on the back, his expression less cold now. "Are you quite all right?"

Fara offered a fresh mug of what smelled like clean water. "Sorry, my lady. They must have a hot sauce over them. I didn't know. The staff didn't say anything when they set the tray on the table."

"It's delicious, actually. I just wasn't prepared."

Fara stood, hands fisting at her sides. "I'll take care of this." She stormed away.

Panicking, Tahlia pointed at the two and the five. "That'll be my choices. Forgive me, I need to stop my squire from murdering an innocent seafood server."

She started to stand, but Marius took hold of her wrist with an iron grip. With a gasp, she stopped. What was he doing?

He blinked, seemingly confused by his own actions. "Apologies. Do go. So sorry."

Tahlia nodded and took off, scanning the crowd

of servants for one who was being destroyed by a well-meaning maniac.

But her mind was elsewhere, playing a game with a handsome, dangerous male she had no business thinking about.

CHAPTER 16
MARIUS

Marius left Titus to the gaming board, giving some lame excuse about needing to speak to Remus concerning a saddle issue. He was feeling... All wrong. Irritated. Agitated. Frustrated. Hot. Confused. He rubbed a hand over his face and tried to decide where he was going.

Outside. Yes. Some air would help.

The lowering sun gilded the outside of the keep and turned all the crystals into mirrors for the sky's tattered clouds. He braced his forearms on the half wall that opened to the area leading to the cliff's edge, the spot where they often took off at the start of a mission.

A hum of energy rolled over his shoulders, down

his torso, and then lower. He frowned. What was that? He'd felt something odd in the arena this morning too. Even Ragewing had noticed it, so he wasn't completely losing his mind. Or was he going mad, and the dragon had simply been humoring him? After all, one small female with an overactive mouth had completely discombobulated him.

What was that shade her cheeks turned when she blushed? It was almost the color of autumn crystal wine... He shook his head and finished his mug of watered wine. So foolish.

A subtle wash of light caught his eye. He looked toward the cluster of varied crystals that grew in the rock over the keep's entrance archway. Had they lit up? Surely not. That would mean their magic was working...

A light, feathery sensation danced down him and brought his body to a version of alertness that was highly unacceptable at the moment.

"I am sorry for saying what I did about your face, High Captain."

His heart slammed into his ribs. Stones and snakes and everything in between, it was the female. Why was she following him? And why did her leathers fit her unlike how they fit anyone else?

"If you stare at my waist for much longer, I'm

going to think you appreciate it more than my ability to ride a dragon," she said, grinning like an Unseelie.

His body thrummed with want. What was happening?

She sidled up to him and leaned against the half wall. Her golden amber eyes almost appeared glazed.

"Did you have stronger wine? I assure you that the sky battle to come is no small thing. You must be in top shape if you plan to display your talent on the dragon and with fire commands..."

Her gaze snared him, and his words of warning fizzled on his tongue. The world tipped a little.

He reached out and tucked a loose strand of her ebony hair behind her gently pointed ear. She shivered and her eyes half shut.

"You're fascinating." He was in a daze... "So fearless."

A grin slicked across her wine-damp lips and he longed to taste the drink on them. Another wave of desire lashed through him.

Her eyes snapped open wide and her grin broke into a bright smile. "Ah, no. I do feel fear. But my passion overrides it. To feel the wind as we fly... The dragons are miracles! The way they work with us instead of eating us whole. They could and well we know it. And their ability to turn and soar and dive. Don't get me started about their beautiful flame!"

Her joy suffused him. She understood what he felt for dragons and for the sky. She, unlike anyone, displayed the happiness he felt quietly inside...

Suddenly his hands were tangled in her wavy hair and he was pressing his lips against hers. She tasted like spice and wine and warm summers. He gripped her waist—so small in the circle of his hands. His blood roared and he shoved her against the half wall. She laughed, low and sultry, against his mouth and twisted her tongue with his. Sensations like sparks lit up his skin at every point of contact.

"Oh, no..." Ophelia's voice cut through the fog stirring Marius's mind. "I guess you two didn't get the warning in time."

Jerking backward, he clasped Tahlia's hips tightly. Stones, he had kissed Tahlia, and Ophelia had seen them.

Tahlia quickly stepped away from him and shook her head. "I'm sorry. I don't know what happened. I promise you that—"

Ophelia held up a hand. "Calm yourself, competitor. It's the crystals. A series of small earthquakes in the valley lit up the ley lines, and the breeding crystals activated. They have been flashing off and on since this morning, though only one guard noticed and he thought he was mistaken."

Tahlia was still flushed and a tangle of hair hung over one luminous eye. "Activated. Without a dragon's touch?"

"Yes," Ophelia said. "They warned us inside, but I guess you two missed the announcement... Anyhow, be careful. If you felt the effects that strongly, the magic will likely give you some tempestuous imaginings. They mean nothing."

Marius felt like he was under a scribe's eyeglass. "Yes, I was getting some air and, well, I, it was certainly disconcerting." He took a breath to steady himself, then bowed once to Ophelia and once to Tahlia. "Though the explanation makes this incident understandable, I remain apologetic. To you both. Now, I must meet with Remus before the sky battle preparation begins."

He spun on his heel and strode through the courtyard toward the gate, his mind on the wrong pair of lips.

The sunset's light and mist blurred the view of his pathway. Dizzy, he wound his way toward the southern wing's side entrance.

His thoughts refused to be tamed as he imagined a disrobed Tahlia lying on her stomach at the edge of the cliff, near the takeoff point. Moss cushioned her naked body and he couldn't stop staring at the way her legs curved up to her...

He blinked and tried to dispel the daydream as he climbed a curving set of stone steps. But his mind wouldn't obey and instead showed him Tahlia.

In the moss at the edge of the cliff, she glanced over her shoulder, her pouty lips swollen from kissing him. He covered her bare body with his and whispered in her ear.

"Wild one, I have caught you now."

She moaned and shifted one smooth leg so that he was positioned to fully mate with her. Pressing her hands to the earth with his fingers laced in hers, he held her in place and drove into her warmth. A groan escaped him and he forced himself to go slowly, though the feel of her was breaking him into glorious, blissful pieces. She called his name and he lowered himself—nearly losing his control—to nibble the tip of her ear. She shivered beneath him.

"More, Marius. More. Now..." She turned and he savored the side view of her face, her shuttered eyes and dark lashes. Her sweet tongue touched her bottom lip.

His body tightened and he almost finished then and there, but he kept himself in check, arms shaking as he thrust strong but still slow, drawing her into a fury of mewling sounds and gasps.

"Please."

Her pleas were a tonic stronger than any wine. He couldn't believe he had this courageous, beautiful, sun ray of a female...

She cried out, hips bucking as much as they could, pinned as he had her, and he increased his pace until all was pleasure—and the only good kind of pain—in a breath-stealing release.

Marius blinked and opened his eyes. Somehow, he had made it back to his bedchamber. He stood, slightly dizzy, with his cock in his hand. He pressed his forehead against his bedpost. It had been a daydream. He was the biggest fool ever to fly a dragon, but he couldn't quite bring himself to regret the imagining.

"You're pulling me apart, Tahlia of Northwoods," he whispered to the empty room. "Absolutely destroying me."

CHAPTER 17
TAHLIA

ertainly disconcerting? Tahlia marched across the courtyard and pushed through the great hall doors. The rest-time festivities were ongoing like something insane hadn't just occurred. First off, what kind of phrase was that—*certainly disconcerting?* She growled and rolled her eyes. Second, that kiss had been far more than disconcerting. It had been...heart-rending. The way his arms had felt around her, the honey and clove scent of him, the urgency of his hands, and how he'd looked at her like she was the center of his world...

But Ophelia had spoken the truth, and now that the crystals had calmed and Tahlia could draw her mind away from that energy, she felt that truth. The kiss had been only a product of the breeding magic of the rose-hued crystals. It hadn't been real. And it was good it wasn't a true kiss. If the rumors were true, Marius was engaged. To Commander Gaius's daughter, no less!

Tahlia rubbed her face and tried to forget the feel of his breath on her cheek and the press of his hard body against hers.

"Where in all the realms have you been?" Fara rushed up, wringing her hands. "After that announcement, I worried you'd run off with a stable hand."

"Would have been a better choice, believe me." Tahlia hurried toward the corridor that led to the baths. She had to clear her head and wash all of that distraction off of her.

"What are you talking about?"

"We kissed," Tahlia whispered as they turned a bend.

A colored-glass sconce flickered with fire on the wall beside them.

Fara made a sound that made Tahlia wonder if she was about to turn inside out. "You, you what?!"

"You heard me." Tahlia took another turn and began to descend the steps to the lower levels of the keep.

Fara was on her heels. "The High Captain?"

"Shh!"

"Shh is right!" Fara grunted, gasped, and muttered a string of curses. "Does this mean that his engagement is off?"

"Hush, please. No, it doesn't. The crystals were the reason."

"Oh. Right."

"Lady Ophelia saw us."

"May monkeys fly from my—"

Tahlia spun and clapped a hand over Fara's mouth. She smiled to soften the attack. "Please, let this go. I shouldn't have even told you. It was nothing."

Fara's eyebrow twitched. "Your look says it was definitely something," she mumbled through Tahlia's hand. "He's going to kick you out, isn't he?"

Rolling her eyes, Tahlia continued into the bathing chambers. They were delightfully empty. "No, he wouldn't do that. He's a good male. I mean, I think he is. That whip is somewhat concerning... But I'd say he is a very good person."

"And you know that because you two are so close?"

"I am not in love with your tone."

"I'm not in love with you risking that scary

female's wrath for a quick roll in the hay with the most dangerous male on the mountain!" Fara whisper-shouted.

"Please with every cake in all the realms and every cherry created in the entire universe on top, stop talking."

Squeezing her eyes shut momentarily, Fara nodded. "Fine. But if anyone tries to hurt you, I'm going to...to rip their heads from their shoulders and kick them off the cliffs and—"

"Fara."

She swallowed and took a breath. Pinching her lips with thumb and forefinger, Fara acted as if she were turning a lock and key.

"Thank you," Tahlia said quietly. "I don't think beheading Mist Knights should ever be on the to-do list."

Fara grumbled but kept her threats mostly silent.

The female competitor chamber was also empty and Tahlia was soon in the hot-spring-fed water, attempting to wash away the event. Fara kept quiet as she too washed up, but the looks she cast Tahlia were loaded with fears. Her friend saw too much.

THE SKY WAS a haze of sundown-hued mist. The Seabreak under Tahlia flew like she was swimming, her spine rolling as she maneuvered within the formation of their battle team.

"Don't let him blaze me!" Ophelia shouted at Tahlia.

Ophelia was only on Tahlia's side of the mock sky battle because the commander had drawn names in the arena before takeoff. Perhaps it was a stroke of luck instead of the catastrophe the dark side of Tahlia's mind suggested. Ophelia was amazing on her Green-flanked Terror, all confidence, decisiveness, and smooth maneuvers. But the way she directed her dragon was not good, and Tahlia had bitten her tongue more than once already, wishing she could tell her to stop with the harsh treatment.

Ophelia hammered a fist into the Terror's shoulder. She had on these spiked gloves that even a dragon such as hers would suffer from. At some point, Tahlia would have to figure out a way to get those things from her when they landed and toss them off the side of the mountain.

The Terror shrieked but obeyed the command, turning sharply among the red-tinged clouds to face their mock enemies flying toward them in the distance—Marius, Titus, and numbers three, four, six, and seven.

Tahlia and Ophelia's team consisted of the rest of the competitors—one, two, eight, and nine. Ten and eleven had dropped out quietly after seeing their flying scores. It was surprising that four and his Spikeback had returned. Admirable, certainly.

"Remember," Ophelia called out to their team with her Mistgold voice, "five goes in for short bursts of flame to break their formation."

Tahlia leaned over her Seabreak's cyan-colored neck, aiming her voice for the dragon's ears. "You ready, darling?" The dragon shuffled its second set of wings. "You're gorgeous, you know that?" The Seabreak lifted its snout in recognition.

"One and two," Ophelia continued, the wind tearing at her blue-green plaits, "you herd the half on the right side lower down while eight and nine herd the other half to a higher altitude. Keep them busy until I can blast them each with a mock stream that would take them out in a true fight."

They were permitted to use sparks or third fire, a lesser flame that would wound but not kill in most cases.

Ophelia's bright blue gaze found Tahlia, and Tahlia felt the look like a jab to the throat.

She swallowed. "Aye, Captain!"

The rest echoed Tahlia's call and they increased speed, heading toward Marius and his team.

Ophelia gripped her dragon's sides with the gold and copper claw-shaped tips of her terrible gloves. That had to hurt. Why did she feel she needed to control the dragon like that? Weren't they properly bonded?

Oh, they weren't. That brought reason to all of Ophelia's behaviors—the striking and clawing and extreme vicious tone in her commands. Ophelia was afraid. Did the High Captain know? Was her father, the commander, aware?

"Stop daydreaming and get to it, five!"

Ophelia's harsh shout shook Tahlia from her thoughts and she urged the Seabreak into a flight path just slightly above Marius's team.

Marius's gaze was steely and unblinking as she flew over his head.

"Merchant's purse with a goat!" Marius called out to his team.

What in all the realms did that mean?

Before his team could react to the command, Tahlia had her Seabreak shoot sparks at Titus and his Spikeback. Titus and his dragon veered away from the formation as the others on the opposing team began breaking into three groups with one rider falling back—it was number three, a male on another Seabreak.

Turning her dragon, Tahlia urged the Seabreak to rain sparks in Marius's direction.

He moved like a lightning strike, uncoiling his whip and lashing it toward Tahlia. She gasped and drew back, and the Seabreak reared in the misty sky. The tip of the whip had been mere inches from Tahlia's face before she'd moved. He either had perfect aim and was careful not to cut her, or he had missed.

She didn't think the great Shadow of the Shrouded Mountains tended to miss a target. So she winked in thanks for his mercy before blasting him—third fire only, of course. His eyes widened briefly before he steered his scarlet Heartsworn out of the way, flying low to face members of Tahlia's team. Sparks filled the fighting area and lit the misty clouds as Tahlia drove the Seabreak toward another male on another Spikeback. It was number six, not number four, thankfully. She would feel bad attacking four after his and his dragon's injury, but if she had to attack eventually, well, the situation was what it was. This was hardly a happy picnic up here and the weak had to be culled from the group no matter how tough that was to swallow.

The attacked Spikeback roared and Tahlia's Seabreak lunged for the other dragon's throat.

"Mock battle!" Tahlia called to the Seabreak even as her heart thundered in her ears.

But the Seabreak didn't listen. She bit down on the Spikeback's throat and soon both dragons, and their riders, were tumbling through the fighting. Tahlia gripped the saddle with every ounce of strength she possessed. Sparks singed her exposed forearms and her cheeks. Her stomach rose into her throat as they spun over and over.

She had to stop this.

"Call her off!" number six yelled from the Spikeback's saddle.

"Trying!"

But she knew she had to do more than shout commands. She slid off the saddle and used the Seabreak's slender neck spikes to climb along the dragon's neck, her legs wrapped around the beast as best as possible. They didn't have as many spikes as a Spikeback, but they had enough for this terrifying job. The dragon jerked. Tahlia lost hold with one hand. She gasped and clasped tightly with her legs, getting another grip on the dragon's spikes. Once she reached the pressure point in the dragon's throat, she pressed her fist into the Seabreak's softer underside scales.

The dragon shrieked and fell back and Tahlia's legs lost their hold. She dangled off the rearing Seabreak, grasping tightly to the spikes.

"I'm sorry! I had to. You forgot it was a mock fight. Come on, love. Calm down!"

The wind tore at Tahlia's limbs and stole her breath as the Seabreak launched itself above all of the others.

"I have treats if you let me live through this, darling! Cake! So much cake!"

A snarl pealed from the dragon's mouth and she tipped herself to the right. Tahlia scrambled onto the saddle and righted herself. Panting, she grasped the lashing reins and managed to steer the Seabreak back to the sky battle.

"You are getting so much cake!"

Tears of relief and joy burned Tahlia's eyes. This was living. She could never go back to simply cleaning tack and trailing Fae with better blood around the Shrouded Mountains. No, she was well and fully hooked on the life of a Mist Knight.

Number six waved a thanks, his face haggard with fear.

"Get in front of me, five!" Ophelia crowed from the back of her Green-flanked Terror. "We only have Titus and Marius to beat now!"

Her dragon roared and blasted Titus with a spray of third fire intermingled with at least a smattering of fourth fire. Ophelia was pushing the boundaries of the mock status of this fight.

Marius and his Heartsworn rose from a bank of thick clouds and blazed sparks at Ophelia and Tahlia. Tahlia urged her Seabreak to fly below Marius and then had the dragon whip its tail upward to smack the underside of the Heartsworn. Marius's dragon let out a broken snarl. A flurry of movement blurred before Tahlia's eyes and suddenly Marius and his dragon were flying alongside her and her Seabreak. Marius's whip slithered through the space between them and wrapped its end around Tahlia's wrist.

Her blood ran cold. Did she truly know him? Of course, she didn't. Fara had been right. He could rip her from her seat and toss her to the earth in a moment.

Keeping her legs tight on the Seabreak, Tahlia used her free hand to grab the whip and she twined it around her saddle's pommel.

"Dive!" she ordered her dragon.

The Seabreak dove like a falling star toward the arena, dragging Marius and his Heartsworn with them.

Marius released the whip, and the handle bounced along the wind currents to lob the Seabreak in the side. She snorted and Tahlia pulled the dragon out of the dive and urged her back toward Ophelia. Marius, without his whip, had his dragon surge after Tahlia and the chase was on.

Heartsworns and Seabreaks were the two fastest types of dragons, so they were matched there. Heartsworns could only blaze flame a few times a day, while Seabreaks could blow fire twice as often even if the flames weren't as powerful.

Since she had far less experience with tactics, this was Tahlia and her dragon's only advantage.

Surely, Marius's mount was out of fire for the day. In the rules read before the mock battle, she'd learned that the riders had to mimic true abilities. Marius couldn't have his dragon blaze them if the dragon would normally be out of fire for the day.

Tahlia tugged a rein and pressed her leg into the dragon, turning sharply in the bracing wind. She bumped the Seabreak's shoulder five times and the dragon let loose a shower of sparks that just kept going.

Marius's Heartsworn was forced to fall back and act as if he had been seriously injured.

Ophelia cheered from above as she flew beside an obviously defeated Titus and the rest of the competitors still airborne.

Marius flew downward, toward the arena, but he glanced at Tahlia over his shoulder. "You owe me a whip!" His voice was harsh, but the corners of his lips twitched as if he was fighting a grin.

She wanted to be hopeful, but had her loss of dragon control ended her dream of becoming a Mist Knight? Controlling one's mount was the most important part of the job, and number six's Spike-back bore the evidence of her failure in a nasty, ragged bite along the beast's throat. Granted, the dragon was still flying and the wound wasn't bleeding too much. But would that be enough to claim the loss of control wasn't significant? Though Tahlia was a determined optimist, even she knew that was doubtful.

They landed and Commander Gaius stormed toward Tahlia.

CHAPTER 18
TAHLIA

Was he going to run her through right here for all to see? Well, that was better than being roasted by a dragon, wasn't it? Perhaps not. It would have been interesting to see the inside of dragon fire before death.

His features unreadable, Marius swallowed and stepped closer to Tahlia. Was he going to attempt to shield her from whatever was headed her way via the commander's sword or fist?

"You are a wonder!" Commander Gaius grabbed her shoulders and gave her a shake.

Shock almost stole her voice. Almost. "I am?"

He shook her again, grinning like a madman.

Her hair fell further out of the tight braids Fara had worked into her hair after the bath.

"You are."

The assembly cheered from the stands and the king and queen addressed them as the Mist Knights and the other competitors gathered around the commander and Tahlia. Noise covered their conversation and the crowd seemed happy enough to shout well wishes to the royals, who headed toward the festivities that would begin in the outer bailey now that the tournament's events were complete. Only the announcement of the winner had yet to happen.

"She left formation," Ophelia said quietly, gaze on her father. Their hair was an exact match. "She lost control of her mount."

Tahlia held out a hand toward Ophelia. "She speaks the truth. I can't deny that."

"Oh, yes," Commander Gaius said, "you were terrible during most of the battle. But the stones you have, Lady Tahlia!"

"You mean breasts, maybe?"

He glanced down and frowned before waving off her words and throwing an arm around her shoulders. "The type of courage I just witnessed, well, that is what we need up there, and if I were a gambler, my gladecoin would be on you winning this thing. I am quite glad that I don't need to make the difficult decision as to who wins the tournament. That job belongs to my future son-in-law."

So it was true—Lady Ophelia and High Captain Marius were engaged. A strange twisting sensation ran through Tahlia's stomach. The other Mist Knights and competitors murmured congrats awkwardly and continued complimenting one another's flying and talking excitedly about all that had gone on up there in the misty sky.

The king and queen made their way through the bowing and curtseying crowd.

Tahlia curtseyed alongside a bowing Marius, who had joined her and Gaius.

King Lysanael's green eyes flashed with delight. "Wonderful match."

Marius nodded. "Thank you, Your Majesty."

Ophelia strutted over, making eye contact with everyone except Tahlia. She took Marius's arm.

Commander Gaius rubbed his hands together and raised his eyebrows. "How about we get cleaned up for the announcement feast? A great many festivities await us tonight. High Captain, do you have a winner set in your mind yet?"

"Not yet. There is much to consider."

"Yes, of course. Always practical and stern, our Marius is," the commander said quietly to the king and queen. He clapped Marius on the shoulder.

Marius's squire, Remus, broke through the ragged group of riders and bowed low. "May I speak with my lord?"

Queen Revna smiled at him. "Rise and do as you see fit, squire."

Remus whispered quickly in Marius's ear. The High Captain's expression went blank.

"Remus, wash down Ragewing," he ordered quietly, his gaze distant, "and give him two scoops of the gold meal." He pressed his eyes shut for a moment.

"Aye, sir."

He gave Remus a nod then hurried away.

Fara slipped through the group and up to Tahlia as Albus and the other healers broke the party apart and began tending to cuts and minor burns. The dragons were being tended to behind them and the crowd had mostly dispersed.

"I'm so glad I was in the latrine during what people are calling your courageous act," Fara whispered.

"Why were you in the latrine? Tell me you weren't so worried that I would die that it made you sick. Tell me it was the asparagus they served during rest time."

Fara snorted. "I would if I could, my lady, but asparagus never gave me Tahlia-level anxiety."

"Asparagus is good like that. Eh, do you have any idea what Marius's squire just told him?"

"No. What happened? Where is the High Captain? Maybe it's something about the queen's dragon, Arkyn."

"Why do you say that?"

"Arkyn took the last hour of the tournament to invade the kitchens."

"Oh, dear."

"More like *oh, blueberries*. Even part of the great hall is tracked with dragon footprints."

Tahlia politely declined a healer's attention and tried to be excited for the coming pronouncement. Would it be her? Could she dare to hope?

"Do you have any cake?" she asked Fara.

"How did you know?" Fara pulled a small pink circle from her pocket. "Never mind. Dumb question." She handed it over. "I've had more than enough, so eat the whole thing, Lady Tahlia. Please."

"Oh, it's not for me."

Tahlia hurried to where the stable hands and healers were tending to the dragons. Her Seabreak tossed her head and snorted at Tahlia's approach. Fara took the Seabreak's reins from one of the hands and held the dragon loosely as Tahlia offered up the treat to the dragon.

"I promised," Tahlia said to the Seabreak. "And I don't break my promises."

The dragon sniffed the cake and glanced at a stable hand, who was eyeing them judgmentally.

Tahlia rubbed the Seabreak's cyan side. "Ignore him. You compromised up there with me and I insist you enjoy a special dessert."

Finally, the dragon nibbled the cake from Tahlia's palm. The beast's lips tickled her skin and she felt as though her face might crack from grinning too much. She set her forehead against the Seabreak's and both of them exhaled.

"Thanks again for not dropping me to my death. I know my inexperience was an issue."

The great creature snuffled against her neck, blowing back her messy black waves.

"Wish me luck in there, all right?"

The Seabreak huffed a hot breath that smelled of fire, and that was about as good as one could get for a well-wish from a dragon.

"...and if she wanted your opinion, she would

give it to you!" Fara was waving a fist at the judgmental stable hand.

"Will you bring her back to the stables?" Tahlia asked Fara. "I'll meet you inside."

"As you say, my lady." Fara gave the stable hand a glare and led the Seabreak the same way Remus had already directed Ragewing to go.

Tahlia looked around as she began the short walk to the great hall. Marius was still notably absent and most of the Mist Knights and competitors had already left for the announcement. Heart beating in her mouth, Tahlia walked on, heading closer and closer to the moment that would either make or break her dreams.

CHAPTER 19
MARIUS

In his chamber, Marius flexed his hands at his sides as his valet unlaced his leather vest. His valet quickly dressed him in a dark blue tunic trimmed in gold thread, black trousers, and black boots. His valet brushed his hair out and tied it back in a simple queue.

"That's fine. Thank you." Marius urged his valet to take the rest of the night off. He had no patience for any more fussing. Plus, there was little time for it.

His mind threw out images of Tahlia flying, her small body poised expertly on her dragon like she'd been born in the saddle. The light in her eyes that turned to fire when she focused on the mock enemies... She was a wonder. Gaius was right to be awed and to make note of her courage.

His mind wove images of memories that had never happened. He threw Tahlia on his bed and she let her knees fall open. Her skin glimmered in the candlelight and the soft spot halfway up her thigh tasted like salt and sugar. A surge of want cascaded through him, heating him to an unbearable degree. He imagined crawling on top of her and binding her wrists to the headboard with his whip. Swallowing, he could almost see the way her head dropped back as she moaned and closed her eyes as he drove into her, showing her that she was his and his alone.

Smashing a fist into the plaster between the stones of his bedroom wall, he snarled.

His mind was a terrible master. Those things would never happen. Of course they wouldn't. But he had to break his engagement with Ophelia. It was quite clear he couldn't be loyal to her. Not after the way Ophelia had begun treating her dragon. She never would have done that when she first signed on. He'd spoken to her about the rough behavior toward the creature numerous times. And also, he couldn't ignore the way his body—and his heart— had been inspired by Tahlia. Even if the worst happened, the engagement had to end.

Crashing into the chair at his desk, Marius leaned forward and gripped his head. His chest shuddered. He would fail Bellona, his beloved sister.

I just can't do it, Sister. Can you forgive me? I will still be the best Mist Knight I can, but this, I can't do this. Ophelia's bloodline is ideal, but the situation is not what I'd thought... Nothing is as I had thought it was. His throat was thick and he gritted his teeth.

Nothing was going according to plan. Absolutely nothing.

I'm so sorry I have failed you, Bellona.

Marius went to his desk and reread the message that Remus had reported. He crushed the parchment in his fist and growled. *Damn it, Tahlia.* He pressed his fist against his forehead and wished there were some way out of this. But rules were rules for a reason. And he had dedicated his life to the Order of the Mist Knights.

Shaking his head, he threw the note to the floor and stormed out of his chamber.

CHAPTER 20
TAHLIA

Tahlia gasped as Marius showed up beside her, silent as death. In line for a refill of the dark wine pouring from the crystal fountain, she nearly dropped her goblet. Fara was already saving her a seat in the middle of the table near the western-facing hearth.

"Yes, High Captain? Aren't you supposed to be up there?" She nodded toward the front of the hall where the king, queen, and Commander Gaius ate at a small table separate from the two other long tables.

"I must speak to you. Privately."

"You look even stormier than usual." She was teasing him, but the steel in those eyes made her shiver. It was not an altogether unpleasant sensation.

He didn't rise to her barb and instead took off out the door, not even watching to see if she would follow. Of course, she did trail him. What was happening? Was this good or bad? She tried to glance at Fara before leaving the great hall, but there were too many servants going this way and that, blocking her view.

Outside, the half-moon had risen like a scythe in the black sky. The heads of the Seabreak and two other dragons showed in the area between the courtyard and the arena. The stable hands were giving the dragons one last walk before sleep, most likely. Marius led Tahlia to a shadowed corner between the keep's western face and the wall that ran along the courtyard to the arena and the cliff launching point.

Not thirty yards away, he had grabbed her and kissed her hard. Just there. Where the moonlight now cascaded across the rock wall and over the hand-trimmed grass of the courtyard. She could almost feel his fingers digging into her hips. A pulse of warmth between her thighs made her stop before joining him fully in the shadows. The moon's silver luminescence cut across his cheekbones, and his brow shaded his unblinking eyes. Hands fisted at his sides and body coiled, he looked ready for a fight.

A chill wrapped her in a frosty cloak of doubt.

"Tahlia. I know..." His focus dropped to her boots, and then he looked up again and met her gaze. "...about your blood."

Her heart hammered in her ears and she dropped back a step. "What?"

"When Albus cut you to test for ghostmint hiding in your veins, the Bloodworkers examined your blood." His eyes squeezed shut, then opened again, and he pinched the bridge of his nose. "That's how you were able to lie. Did you lie about how long you trained at Grimsbrook? I can't believe I was so foolish. You lied to me. I thought we understood one another. I thought I'd found someone that actually felt the same way I do about..." He gestured to the sky and shook his head, his jaw clenching.

He meant about flying and dragons, about the life of a Mist Knight. "You did. I do. You can't be angry."

"Oh, really? I can't. How does that work out? Actually, don't bother saying anything. Every word from your lips could be a lie, human."

"I'm half-human and it doesn't matter because I am meant for this. You know it as well as I do."

"I know nothing about you."

"Did that taste sour? That had to be a stretched truth. You know everything important. I can fly with the best of them. You, Ophelia, Titus, the other Seabreak rider I saw up there taking scores."

"Maiwenn."

"Yes, I'm as good as her too. You know that about me. You know that I care about the other riders on my team and I care about the dragons. That's more than I can say for your intended mate."

Wincing, he looked away for a moment. "I have seen those new gloves of hers. She has always been too rough on her dragon. I will confiscate the gloves. Now, stop. Stop talking. We aren't discussing Ophelia."

"Are you going to sentence me to death?"

He lifted his head, exposing his throat. "What choice do I have?"

"Does that mean you don't want to?"

Shifting his focus to her face, he stared, silent. She wondered again how he had received the scar that ran along the side of his handsome visage.

"I'm not the one who did the testing. The Bloodworkers know the truth about you. This cannot be kept secret. Not for long."

"What do you mean?"

"I mean, you must flee, Tahlia. Run back to wherever you call home. Or somewhere else. Anywhere but in the Shrouded Mountains."

"I was born in the valley. I'm not human in any real sense of the word. All I know is Fae. And dragons." Unshed tears burned her eyes and they turned her foul blood to flame in her heart. "I will not run from who I am. I am a dragon rider and I am your next Mist Knight."

"All you will be is a pile of ash if you don't escape this place within the next hour." His gaze had turned pleading, his eyebrows lifted and his hands almost reaching for her, though he kept back just inches from touching her.

"Knights don't run from a challenge. They fly toward it."

He lunged, startling her, and he grabbed her arms in a viselike grip. "You must go, Tahlia. Please. I'm already breaking my oath by telling you this and giving you this one chance. I have never, ever broken a rule of the Knights. You with your wild joy and your ridiculous courage have bent my resolve like a storm tosses a willow."

"You're the storm." Like her fingers belonged to someone else, her forefinger found his scar and traced its path from temple to jawline.

He shivered and shut his eyes. "And you light the skies like a second sun and grow happiness in the cold ground of my heart."

Her soul ached. Her heart beat hard and slow— once, twice. She put her palms over her chest and tried to breathe evenly. She would fall right into the storm that was Marius Leos Valentius, Shadow of the Shrouded Mountains, and delight in every shock of thunder and lash of rain...

When his slitted, gray-black eyes flashed open, his lips parted.

She imagined him crushing her to him. His kiss would taste like his scent—of cloves and honey— and he wouldn't set his lips on hers gently, but like a powerful male who wanted to claim her as his own. His hands would cup her face roughly; his tongue would tangle with hers.

At just the imagined scenario, fierce longing shot through her like a bolt of lightning. What was it about this proud, stern male that attracted her so? But she knew already. It was the way he treated his dragon, how he had helped her quietly along this extraordinary journey, and the fatherly protectiveness he displayed for his knights in the sky. Even if it was madness, she wanted this male.

If they could be together...

Every inch of her would hum with desire. She imagined the many sensations she'd feel in his arms... The turn of his shoulder muscles under her fingers. The groan slipping from his mouth as he kissed his way down her neck to her chest. They would fall to the ground and he would take her here in the shadows with desperate movements, like touching one another would save them both somehow from whatever consequences this connection threw at them as well as the very real danger that awaited her inside the hall.

But all of that was only in Tahlia's head. He stood gripping her arms hard enough to bruise.

With a growl, he pushed away from her. His hair was wild and his eyes wilder. "Go, Tahlia. Please. Just leave. I can't..."

She couldn't leave this place or give up. If she did, the fire inside her would die and she would be a husk of her former self. She wouldn't be Tahlia any longer.

"I will face the consequences. Do what you must do, High Captain. Now, I have an announcement to attend."

He shut his eyes once more, and she glanced at him one last time before leaving him in the moonlight. His hands flexed at his sides and his breaths came too quickly. Forcing herself to keep on walking, she found the door, swung it open, and prepared to meet her fate, whether it be fine fortune or death by a dragon's blaze.

CHAPTER 21

TAHLIA

Tahlia found Fara wielding an eating knife and threatening an elderly male. "I told you I was saving this seat. Now, back off. I don't care what kind of military background you have, you old cod! I'll cut it right out of you!"

Lowering her friend's weapon, Tahlia eased Fara away from the table. "Eh, I need to tell you something."

Once she had, Fara's purple skin turned nearly gray. "I knew this would happen. I can have Daffodil ready in fifteen minutes. Meet me by the outer bailey gate."

"I'm not running, Fara."

"Of course you are."

"Am I a fearful sort?"

"No, but this is no time for your brand of courage, which I deem madness even at the best of times and this isn't that."

"What?"

"Nothing. You are leaving. We are leaving. We will keep our flesh unsinged and call this a grand adventure. I hear the human settlement of Deigs is an open-minded city where two Fae could find a way to live."

"I'm not leaving. You go. I want you to go and be safe. I'm facing this. I would rather die than flee. I am meant for this. I am a Mist Knight."

Fara twisted her hands and spoke close to Tahlia's face, so close that she could smell her friend's wine on her breath. "You have the heart of one, but sadly, you don't have the blood. We can't change their minds. It's a rule and Mist Knights are more obsessed with rules than they are their dragons."

"Go. Please," Tahlia said. The echo of Marius's warning gripped her heart, a trembling hold that threatened to shake her into pieces.

Not waiting for Fara to argue, Tahlia pivoted and strode to the front of the hall where the other competitors were lining up for the announcement.

Commander Gaius walked in from a side door

with Ophelia. The commander raised his arms to quiet the hall.

"I've asked Queen Revna to announce the winner since our High Captain is not in attendance. Please stand."

The queen broke away from her dragon and the king. They had been talking closely with a group of liveried stewards. She walked slowly to the center of the line of competitors, her gaze measuring each of them.

Did she know already?

Tahlia's stomach rolled and she breathed through her nose to keep from being sick all over the queen's fantastic scarlet high-top boots.

"The winner is..."

The queen's gaze traveled over each of the competitors. Number one scratched the scar where his ear had once been. Two and three held as still as statues. Four glanced at Tahlia and nodded—whatever that meant. The rest shuffled their feet or pursed their lips.

"Our new Mist Knight of the Shrouded Mountains, noble protector of the Realm of Lights and the northern coast, is Lady Tahlia of Northwoods!"

Tahlia's heart soared. She felt like she could take flight like a dragon, spreading wings and breathing flame into the clouds. The Bloodworkers hadn't come forward. All was gold and happiness.

I did it. I am a dragon-riding knight. Even if it doesn't last, I did it.

The hall erupted in cheers and most of the competitors gave Tahlia encouraging smiles while a few grimaced, their disappointment understandable.

Commander Gaius and Ophelia stepped forward, and King Lysanael whispered something in Queen Revna's ear. She whispered back and they seemed to have a nearly silent argument, complete with hand-waving and scowls and a growl or two.

"I'm afraid there has been a mistake," the commander said. "Tell us what you found, Head Bloodworker."

Tahlia swallowed. This was it. The end. A sheen of sweat covered her forehead and she fisted her hands to keep her fingers from shaking.

An ashen-faced Marius came through a side door and stared at her. His hair was mussed and his eyes had a feral glaze to them.

A male in Mist Knight livery cleared his throat and read from a parchment. "Competitor five's blood has less than point four percent Mistgold—"

The crowd gasped, but they hadn't even heard

the worst of it. Sweat rolled down Tahlia's back, but she remained standing, holding her head high. She was a Mist Knight, even if her blood wasn't what they wanted it to be.

The Head Bloodworker held up the parchment and the room quieted once more. "Her blood also shows that she is half-human."

Angry shouts burst from several Mist Knights as well as competitors two, three, nine, and seven.

"Mist Knights must be Fae and Fae alone!"

"Mountain dragons don't bond with humans. It's a simple fact!"

"Aye. It would never work."

"A disgrace!"

"Must humans stick their greedy hands into all of our traditions?"

This last bit was whispered by a squire close to Tahlia. The coward would never say such a thing loud enough for the queen and king to hear.

Ophelia locked eyes with Tahlia and grinned.

Tahlia's not-good-enough blood boiled in her veins. She clenched her fists and longed to become the dragon she had felt she was only a few moments ago.

Commander Gaius's eyebrows bunched and his lips turned down at the edges. He motioned at two guards standing at the main doors of the hall. "Based on the evidence, sadly, competitor five is sentenced to death by dragon fire."

A chill swept down Tahlia's body and she fought a shiver. She hoped Fara was long gone, safely away from here.

After more shouting and calls for proof and bumping and shoving, the guards had Tahlia and were roughly escorting her out of the great hall.

The competitors, knights, and some of the squires and servants trailed them out of the keep, across the courtyard, and beyond the wall where Marius had kissed her. The manicured grass of the area leading to the cliff's edge was too lovely to be a place where people died. Faeberries grew along the border of the arena wall and mistblooms with their delicate white petals nodded their heads in the breeze.

Suddenly, Fara was beside Tahlia. "You're looking at the flowers, aren't you? You truly are mad." Tears gleamed in Fara's eyes.

Panic sewed Tahlia's throat shut. She coughed and the guards gripped her arms more tightly, shoving Fara out of the way.

"What are you doing here?" Tahlia whispered. "You must go."

The guards rotated Tahlia around to face those filtering into the grassy area to watch her death. The taller of the two guards began to tie her wrists.

"I'm not leaving you, my lady," Fara said.

Tahlia memorized the slant of Fara's nose and the intense love in her gaze. "You must. I love you, my friend. Go. Now."

Fara wiped a tear with the back of her hand and growled. "No. I won't."

The guard wrapping the rope around Tahlia's wrists paused. "You'll go or you'll be burned alive too, squire."

"I..." Fara sniffed loudly and took a deep breath. "My lady is a true knight and I pledge my loyalty to her."

"No, Fara. Please." Tahlia's heart snapped and pain spread like a crack through her chest. Fara couldn't die. Not yet. Not now.

Marius walked up and clapped the guard on the shoulder. "You're dismissed." He took up the job of tying Tahlia, gently knotting the rope. Then he stood beside her.

Now, Fara and Marius flanked her on either side.

"What are you doing?" Tahlia asked him.

"I, too, believe you are a true knight."

Tahlia's mouth fell open, and though her heart pained her, joy suffused the agony.

Marius's gaze cut to her face, then back to the rope. "Even though you used that half-human tongue of yours to lie to me, I am likewise loyal to you. As a fellow Knight of the Shrouded Mountains."

"Marius, I..." She met his gaze as her mind tried to find the words to explain her absolute satisfaction at earning his loyalty and the horror at him standing by her side in this terrible moment.

"Marius?" Ophelia's voice cracked. "Why?" She stared, her gaze wide and unsure. She looked younger.

He glanced at her, eyes as steely as ever. "I'm no longer your concern."

"But..."

"I won't let a knight suffer this punishment without a show of defiance."

Commander Gaius walked around the crowd to join Ophelia. "A show that will leave you dead. Give this up, High Captain. You've lost your head over this half-human."

The king and queen stood atop a rise of earth at the back of the crowd. An aspen's leaves fluttered over their crowned heads. They were deep in discussion again.

"Marius," Tahlia whispered. "Thank you for believing in me, but please take Fara and go."

"Stand strong, Lady Tahlia," Marius said.

Fara put her hand over Tahlia's forearm. Her fingers were like icicles. "We are with you. No matter what comes."

"Fire is what's coming, Fara." Tahlia's resolve trembled under the weight of these two standing beside her.

A stable hand brought out a dark green Terror. The dragon looked as old as the mountain itself, his scales the dark green of shaded leaves and his eyes like rain-darkened stones. There was no spark of connection in that dragon's gaze as there was in most dragons'. This one had been born deadly and had been bridled to do the worst tasks the Mist Knights required. Trying not to tremble, Tahlia stood her ground. This dragon wouldn't hesitate.

"Go, please. Both of you. Marius, you just met me three days ago. You can't possibly care that much."

"When you face death in the skies together, an hour is enough to feel the bond between knights and I know you are already aware of that fact. Your mercy and courage continue to amaze me and I won't let you die alone. This is wrong, and hopefully, by your actions, your squire's, and my own, the commander will see that before it's too late."

"And I doubt he'll fry his daughter's intended mate," Fara said.

"I am no longer that person."

"You broke it off?" Fara asked.

Tahlia shut her eyes and prayed to the Old Ones. Her heart thundered and cracked. "You have to go. I can't let you die for me." She opened her eyes and bit her lip, wishing with everything inside her that this had all gone differently.

"I ended a relationship that was started for the wrong reasons. I'll explain everything either here if we are spared or in the afterlife if we are so lucky as to be given it."

"Tahlia of Northwoods," Commander Gaius said, his voice monotone, "you are stripped of your false title and deemed a lying human traitor, a blemish on the mountain, undeserving of your time in our ranks." He came closer and rubbed his hand over his face. "Marius," he whispered, "stop this nonsense."

Marius raised his chin and all the emotion left his features. He could have been carved of marble.

A whispering sifted through those gathered to witness Tahlia's death, and then Queen Revna stood beside Ophelia. King Lysanael nodded to Titus and Ophelia and joined his mate.

The stable hand holding the Terror looked to Commander Gaius, who nodded and stepped back, his shoulder brushing his daughter's and his eyes squinted as if he barely wanted to watch.

The stable hand set a fist on the Green-flanked Terror's left foreleg and bumped the scales twice. Blinking and focusing on Tahlia, the Terror raised his head and opened its great maw.

Tahlia held her breath. Fara and Marius took her hands in theirs. Tears pricked at her eyes and her pulse beat the rhythm of a funeral march.

I'm sorry I couldn't send you gold or help you eat like kings, she prayed silently, thinking of her mother and even her less-than-fantastic father. *Old Ones, please bless the souls of these two who stand with me...*

A roaring sounded and the Seabreak Tahlia had ridden flew over the courtyard wall, a stable hand calling out behind her. The cyan-scaled beauty pushed her way past the Terror, who growled low in his throat. The Seabreak put herself between the Terror and Tahlia.

"Stop!" Queen Revna's strong and accented human voice echoed across the courtyard. Why was the king nodding at his mate?

The Terror's stable hand set an open palm on the dragon's shoulder and the beast lowered his head.

"The Seabreak has bonded to her, hasn't she?" The queen gestured toward Tahlia and the female dragon. "You can't deny that. Why would a mountain dragon choose a lesser rider? Mountain dragons are known to be quite particular about their bonds, aren't they?"

"A mountain dragon wouldn't bond with anyone they didn't consider the finest rider," King Lysanael said from where he stood. The cadence of his words said he would brook no argument.

The queen nodded. "And as it turns out, we are privy to information about Lady Tahlia's bloodline that none else here knows. Our informants have discovered that Lady Tahlia's blood comes from a previously unknown Mistgold line."

The ground seemed to shake under Tahlia's boots. What was the queen talking about? That wasn't true. What was she doing? Why was she lying?

Fara glanced at Tahlia. Fara mouthed *keep on praying*. Tahlia did exactly that as the Seabreak leaned over to bump Tahlia's shoulder with her snout.

The Head Bloodworker raised a finger. "Forgive

me, Your Majesties, but the testing performed during Healer Albus's work clearly showed there is very little Mistgold in her blood. We do not simply *eye* the blood and guess."

King Lysanael let out a low growl. "Watch your tone with my mate."

The Head Bloodworker lowered his head and stepped back.

"As I was saying," the queen continued, "the Mistgold in her blood reacts differently than most dragon rider blood. It remains subtle and sometimes mimics that of human blood. They were a line of spies for the royal house. My mate and I, king and queen of this realm, decree this as truth."

They were rescuing her.

Tahlia, despite always being the penultimate optimist, couldn't believe it.

"Your Majesty?" she asked, her voice cracking. She wasn't even sure what she wanted to ask.

Fara grinned wildly, and Marius squeezed Tahlia's fingers, his steely gaze betraying nothing.

The queen smiled at Tahlia. "Release this knight and honor her as the newest member of your order. This is a command, just in case you weren't certain." Queen Revna was human. Was that why she'd saved Tahlia?

Tahlia released a long breath, let go of Fara and Marius, and went to one knee. "Thank you. I will endeavor to make this order and Your Majesty proud."

Queen Revna set a hand on Tahlia's head, and just like that, the moment was over.

The Green-flanked Terror and the Seabreak were taken away and Tahlia was left, wide-eyed and unbelieving, as Marius, Fara, and most of the other knights surrounded her with cheers and well wishes. Marius had disappeared in the crowd, but his voice rumbled through the noise here and there.

Commander Gaius shook her hand, a grim smile on his face. Did he know that Marius had broken off the engagement with Ophelia? It wasn't really her fault, but somehow she felt that it was.

"Welcome to the order, Lady Tahlia," the commander said. "I'm glad your bloodline was found to be suitable." His tone said he knew very well his human queen had been lying through her pretty teeth. "I won't take it easy on you though. Know that."

"Of course not, Commander."

"The king and queen will be gone tomorrow and then I will be fully in charge once more. I do not tolerate deceit or give mercy to those who fall behind in training."

"I understand. There will be no deceit from this day forward."

The commander chewed the inside of his cheek and glanced over her shoulder like he was thinking something through. He seemed less happy by the moment. If pressed, she'd have guessed he was glad such a good rider was in the order but infuriated that she was human. And a liar.

"I'll have to learn to trust your word," he said. "It will take a long while, I imagine."

Tahlia didn't know what to say, so she just gave him a winning smile. He shook his head, seemingly as shocked as she was at the turn of events, then he nodded and walked toward the lights of the great hall.

Fara hugged her tightly as the grumblers who didn't appreciate the queen's interference wandered back into the hall to commence the feasting.

"You did it, Tahlia. You actually changed your fate."

Tahlia squeezed her back. "I couldn't have done it without you." She gazed into her friend's face and Fara's smile echoed her own happiness. "I'll be saying thank you for the rest of my life."

"Seeing as how you like to play with dangerous creatures and their masters, I doubt that you'll be around for very long, but I'll take what I can get."

Tahlia scowled jokingly and hugged Fara again.

Marius strode past a cluster of Bloodworkers speaking to the commander. He held out a hand.

"May I speak to you, Lady Tahlia?"

His tone was cold as usual, but his voice was just like that. It didn't mean he was angry or unfeeling. He was simply...a storm cloud made into a male Fae.

But he had just finished a quiet chat with Commander Gaius, so perhaps he was upset about something aside from the other terrifying events of the day. Ophelia must have left because Tahlia didn't see her anywhere. She had to be livid. Perhaps he had his former intended on his mind?

Despite the shock of how close Tahlia had come to shaking hands with Death, she couldn't help but admire the lovely night. Stars glittered like dragon eyes above them and the wind held the promise of summer. They walked away from the stragglers still in the grassy area, leaving the last of the noise as they entered the empty arena.

"I want to apologize for kissing you."

She shook her head. "It was just the crystals."

"Yes, they were quite powerful at that moment

and we both must be susceptible to such magic." He swallowed and looked away.

"I was definitely susceptible." Still was. But it had nothing to do with crystals.

Clearing his throat, he kept himself a step away from her. "Regardless, I will be certain to refrain from any such behavior in the future."

Tahlia leaned on the wooden fence surrounding the area where she'd fought with her sword.

"Unless I ask for that behavior?" She raised an eyebrow.

A gentle blush covered his sharp cheekbones. "I... Yes, yes. That would be fine."

"So you'd be all right with kissing me right now if I asked you to?"

His gaze cut across her mouth and her breath caught at the ferocious look in his stormy eyes.

"I was just pardoned by the queen and king. That's a pretty good trick, right?" she whispered. "I think I deserve a kiss."

Dimples appeared in his cheeks and he chuckled softly. His hand swept from her shoulder up the back of her neck, giving her wonderful chills. He gripped her head and looked down into her eyes.

"You need to understand what behavior is and is

not permitted when interacting with your High Captain, Lady Tahlia."

"Is this not allowed?" She stood on her tiptoes and brushed her lips over the corner of his jaw.

His throat bobbed in a swallow. "Not at all permitted," he whispered huskily.

Her body warmed. Undoing this stern male was absolutely delightful.

"How about this?"

She slid her hands down his muscular chest and across his flat stomach. His tunic did little to hide the fine lines of his body.

His stomach pulled in as he gasped quietly. "You will be punished for that."

The heat inside her pooled low. "Oh, will I?" Her pulse kicked up, her blood racing.

He slammed her against the fence and kissed her hard, tongue tangling with hers and his fingers in her hair. Tahlia's blood caught fire. She gripped his hips and tugged him close, kissing him back, tasting the honey and clove taste of his mouth and thrilling in every sensation. He pressed into her and she could feel every bit of him. The stars behind his silhouette appeared to spin as he nibbled his way down her neck. She was more than ready for him to toss her down to the arena's sandy ground. Maybe his mouth would find her breasts as she threw a leg over his back...

Someone cleared their throat.

Marius broke away quickly and wiped his mouth. "Yes?" His color was high, but she had no doubt her face was redder.

It was Fara. "I'm so sorry to interrupt, but the knights are asking for you, my lady. The king is looking for you, High Captain."

Tahlia inhaled slowly, trying to stop wanting to throw herself at Marius again despite Fara's presence and the fact that there was a room full of people waiting on them. "Thank you, Fara. We will be in shortly."

Marius gave Fara a nod of thanks and Fara returned to the great hall's pink and golden light.

Tahlia touched Marius's arm and he turned to face her. "Let's enjoy the festivities. We can delight in our own pastimes later this evening."

His eyes glittered dangerously, but the ghost of a grin passed over his mouth. "Agreed."

He looked like a dream she'd had come to life.

"Thank you for believing in me. It's not enough to say *thank you*, but it's all I have."

Taking her hand, he kissed each knuckle. "I'm honored to have aided you, my lady."

Under the blazing stars, Tahlia walked with him into the Mist Knights' great hall. True, she had yet to find out who had poisoned her and there would be hurdles to leap between today and tomorrow, but finally, at long last, she had a home in the place where she truly belonged.

DEAR READERS,

Thank you so much for joining me on this dragon-riding adventure. Sign up for my newsletter at https:// www.alishaklapheke.com/free-prequel-1 for updates on the series.

And grab the next Marius and Tahlia book today!

Kingdom of Spirits

See you around!

Alisha

A QUICK LOOK: THE FAE KING'S ASSASSIN

A sneak peek of another book in the same world as Bound by Dragons...

~Revna of Isernwyrd~

Assassinations and spying had never been my preferred missions. Fights with fists and teeth and steel were refreshingly honest when compared to plotting seduction or slipping herbs into drinks. Which was why I was thankful that my current assignment had nothing to do with gold-hemmed dresses and everything to do with stalking an Unseelie gargoyle through the forest alongside my dragon familiar. I had lost the Unseelie in the heavy underbrush, but the snap of a twig behind me stilled my breath.

I spun and sliced my iron and adamant blade across the gargoyle's abdomen, loosing a stream of smoking black blood. The monster's ratty wings flared wide as he leaped from the brush, lashing a clawed paw at my head. I rolled under his arm, but the Unseelie still clipped my shoulder and I let out a hiss. Pain slithered over the injury. Springing up behind the gargoyle, I gritted my teeth and rammed my sword into its back. The monster fell to the blood-soaked ground.

Steely clouds billowed beside the autumn sun as I stepped over the dead Unseelie monster. Another day, another assignment. And while I might have preferred one mission over another, my master didn't care about my opinion. He owned me in every sense of the word, the curse rune on the back of my neck ensuring my obedience. With one ancient word, he could kill me even from afar. I wiped the gargoyle's stench from my blade and surveyed the skies, seeking a particular pair of dragon wings.

"Where are you, terrible beast?" My dragon, Arkyn, had grown impatient waiting for the gargoyle to show and had flown off to survey the area. Lucky for him, he'd missed the fight. "If you're lolling about in a field of blueberries, I'm going to roast you for my dinner."

Arkyn was a good companion, but he had one weakness. Food.

A shadow blocked the sun, then Arkyn was landing beside me, his color the same hue as the surrounding oak trunks, his eyes as bright as torches, and his wings buffeting me with wind. The dragon was roughly the size of three horses, and when he nudged my stomach, I widened my stance to keep from toppling backward. I rubbed the smooth scales of his head, my heart warming.

"You're lucky I'm still alive." Maneuvering my round shield onto my back, I found a patch of dark moss. I dragged my dirtied sword along the ground to clean it, then I tucked a leg into one of Arkyn's stirrups and hauled my tired arse onto the dragon's back. "No one else would sneak Cook's scraps to your nest. She values those scraps more than all the lives at Isernwyrd."

Arkyn sniffed as if he didn't agree that he had only me to find his favored meal. He spread his bat-like wings and ran over the rocky ground, and we took off. Leaves brushed my boots, and branches tried to snag my cloak as we drove up and away from the forest floor in uneven bursts of forward movement. Above the broken canopy of green, the coming storm blew a chilly wind across my face.

Below, a drumstone's deep blue surface flickered with emerald light and I turned my face toward home. Hopefully, that stone was finished causing trouble for a while. At least long enough for my nap and a meal. I didn't mind the drumstones and the way they spit out Unseelie monsters from hidden realms—killing off things like the gargoyle paid for my keep and gave me coin to save for my ultimate goal. But I needed a day off.

Arkyn flew over the toothlike walls of Isernwyrd. Black pennants snapped from the five towers, the color denoting the Hunters' collective grief over losing the crown princess. The shouts of my fellow Hunters rose as Arkyn landed in the courtyard. Ignoring the other Hunters' kind calls to Arkyn, I slid out of the saddle and ran both hands down the dragon's body, checking for wounds.

"So tell me, was it blueberries or a lady friend?" I made it to his snout and picked a dark blue bit from one of his viciously long canines. Holding it up for him to see, I raised an eyebrow. "Really? I mean, I had guessed... But you truly left me to die for a snack?"

He exhaled a heavy, damp breath into my face, blowing my brown braids back, then bumped me with his snout.

I flicked his nose gently. "You might not believe one gargoyle could have taken me down, but you underestimate my need for a nap."

Wishing the other Hunters would leave us be, I glared at our audience.

"Ah, come off it, Revna." The newest of the Hunters, Cuthnor, a recruit with far more brawn than brains, stalked around Arkyn. His swagger and smirk said he didn't know the story of my dragon and the last arsehat who'd tried his patience. "Let someone else take this beast into the skies. Someone whose strength matches his."

I sighed. I wanted ale and to sit the hells down. "Fine. Let's get this over with." I motioned to Cuthnor. "Take me down and I'll ask Arkyn nicely if he'll take you on a mission. Which he won't."

Cuthnor snorted and tugged at his ragged beard. Inside and out, the man was as ugly as they came. He lunged at me, then went left, trying to take my back. I put out one boot and tripped the fool. With a grace that showed why Master had recruited him this late in life, he caught himself. Normally, we started here as children. Easier to manipulate that way.

Cuthnor grabbed my hair and laughed as he attempted to wrap an arm around my exposed throat. I took hold of the fist tangled in my thick, messy braids, pressed it down onto my scalp to hold him there, and donkey-kicked the moron in the stones. He howled as everyone else guffawed.

"Want another one or are you finished?" I kept both my hands on his fist on the top of my head, not allowing him to use the hold to his advantage.

He let out a few garbled words and spat on the toe of my boot. Fire simmered in my blood.

"These are my favorite boots." I twisted, skipped closer a step, then slammed my heel onto his instep.

He roared and released me to the cackling of the other Hunters.

"It's not the dragon you need on your next job, Cuthnor," the gangly Tynin called out as I used a rag from my pouch to clean spittle from my finely stitched gray leather boots.

Cuthnor stood, still cupping his man bits. "Berserker bitch."

The slur had always pleased me because I took pride in my Berserker blood. I didn't know how many folk still possessed the battle rage magic of my people, but the gift had to be rare. *The king had seen to that,* I thought darkly.

"That's right," I said to Cuthnor. "Don't forget it."

Cuthnor stalked away toward the horse stables as the rest of the Hunters gave me space. I smoothed my hands down Arkyn's belly and unbuckled the saddle. Drawing it over him, I was careful not to clip his wing. Sure, he could handle the pain of a scratched wing, but those lovely appendages were sensitive. I handed the saddle off to a stable boy, then walked alongside Arkyn across the mud-slick cobblestones of the courtyard.

In the sanded square near the entrance to the mess hall, Raulian fought Vi bare-knuckled. Raulian's gaze flicked to me as we passed. Vi knocked him hard with a nice right cross.

"Better focus on the training, Raul." I snorted a laugh.

He came back at Vi with a series of expert strikes. Raulian wasn't the sharpest fellow, but he was a good person and the nearest thing to a friend aside from Arkyn.

Servants in crisp linen aprons and tunics carried baskets of dirtied laundry from the arched doorways of the barracks and into the servants' hall near the chandler's workshop. I'd always thought it ridiculous that Master insisted the servants remain so tidy when he didn't give a rat's foot about what we Hunters looked like.

A shudder rippled through my bones and I swallowed a familiar sour taste on the back of my tongue. Arkyn nudged my shoulder and his tongue darted out to touch my cheek.

"Stop, you little beastie. You know I hate that."

With the sleeve of my tunic, I wiped dragon drool from my face. Though Arkyn's concern over my longstanding full-on fear of Master was sweet, I had no space for it in my life. Hunters had to be cold and show no trepidation—even in front of the man who beat us when we failed in a mission and who controlled the death curse runes inked at the back of our necks.

When we reached the corner of the lower kitchens building, Arkyn lifted his head and sniffed loudly right next to my ear. I shoved him away a step as the scent of freshly baked bread and venison stew filled my nose.

"Don't worry. I'll get you some later." Master would pay me well for killing that monster so quickly. I'd have enough to feed us both for at least two days.

Wide stone steps led up to the abandoned scriptorium, which was now Arkyn's nest. Master had ordered the entrance torn down and a new one crafted of roughly hewn wood, wide enough to permit Arkyn easily. Three slender windows let in some of the approaching storm's metallic breeze and a portion of the day's weak light. Fresh hay sat in a large circle in the back corner of the empty room, along with a trough I filled with water every day before sunrise. Beside that, a wide copper bowl showed the remnants of Arkyn's squirrel and crabapple breakfast, cores and small bones discarded neatly into two piles.

I grabbed the dish and dumped the contents into the rubbish bin that the servants would discard for me later. They did it for free because Master ordered them to keep Arkyn's nest clean. Master didn't give food freely to people, but he did provide a portion for the only dragon Isernwyrd had housed as a Hunter's familiar in two centuries.

A knock sounded behind me and I turned toward the entrance to see Raulian.

"You look even paler than usual." The man was

as fair as a summer's day. Though I hailed from Fjordbok, I wasn't as light-skinned as him.

Raulian pushed his curly white-blond hair away from his face and swallowed. "Master calls for you. The king is here and asking for you."

I dropped the copper dish and it clanged against the flagstone floor, making Arkyn draw back and hiss.

"What? Now?" I hadn't even washed the gargoyle muck off my hands.

"Immediately. Need me to get Arkyn some grub?"

I scratched the only soft spot on my dragon's body—a tiny square of hide behind his ears—then left him with a lazy fist-to-the-chest salute. Starting out of the room, I clapped Raulian on the shoulder.

"Yeah, that would be good. Thanks, Raul. But watch your fingers."

I grinned wickedly and Arkyn took his cue, bristling so that the spear-sharp spikes on his tail fanned out and upward.

"Good dragon," Raul murmured as I left them to it.

I enjoyed teasing Raul, but it was only a weak distraction from the buzzing in my head and the tingling of my fingers. Why was the king here and asking for me? I had never met our ruler. The king always gave his assignments to Master, who then passed them on to whichever Hunter fit the job best.

Hurrying across the courtyard, I eyed the cut on my arm. It wasn't deep, but I needed to clean it soon to avoid infection. Gargoyles were nasty beasts.

Two guards stopped me at the door to Master's chambers. One pointed to my forehead. "You've got Unseelie blood on your face."

"All the better to show him I've been hard at work." I gave the man a nod and he opened the door.

Standing in a pool of sunlight that was as gold as spilled dragon blood, Master spoke in quick whispers to the king. Road dust caked the hem of King Darrew's ruby-red cloak and made his salt-and-pepper hair look brown. He turned as I walked in, his eyes already studying every inch of me.

I didn't know which one I'd rather run through. Both, if my dreams ever came true. I laughed silently at myself and sank into a low bow, my fist against my shoulder in the Hunter fashion, waiting until they spoke to me.

"The dragon Huntress with Berserker blood." The king's voice slid across the chamber's dark stone floor like a snake. His boots sounded his approach while the slap of Master's bare feet marked his movement. "Rise," King Darrew said.

I did so but kept my eyes cast downward. "As you order, my king."

Master poked my ribs with his walking stick. "Show him your ice eyes, Huntress Revna."

Standing perfectly still, I looked at the king, whose eyes flickered with interest. But what kind of interest? A man's lust? A rich man's desire for that which is rare? Or was he only here for a job and my pale blue eyes—the mark of Berserker blood— meant I could do what he needed done?

The king's gaze left my face and found Master's. "Will she do it?"

Master set a heavily ringed hand on his stomach and raised a thick eyebrow. "If you order it so."

"This job will require an especially strong focus to complete successfully and with grace."

"If she doesn't complete this mission, she dies." Master shrugged.

The king smiled and he crossed his arms. "I like the way you work, Master of the Hunters. It's simple. Clean."

"Effective," I said.

Both men's eyes momentarily widened, but respect shone in the king's look. I guessed he would like a show of my bold nature. If he wanted a Berserker, he wanted the death of someone difficult to kill. And he'd come here in the flesh instead of sending a missive. Whatever this job was, it sure wouldn't be a walk down the flowered lane.

"I am your servant, my king." I bowed again. Groveling to these monsters was disgusting, but I had no desire for a beating before my nap and meal.

The tip of Master's stick found my chin and he lifted my head. "Shall I tell her, my king, or do you want to?"

King Darrew's smile turned my stomach. He met my gaze. "You, my rare Huntress, are to kill the King of the Fae."

My mouth fell open and cold swept through me like winter had fallen on Isernwyrd with that one sentence.

My life was over.

I schooled my features, keeping my face blank so as not to show my horror at the king's words. "As you wish, my king."

The king paced Master's chamber. "I'm sure you are aware the crown princess's death was not natural. Someone murdered her."

I could hardly concentrate on his words. Killing the Fae king was impossible. They were sending me to my death. Was it a political move to show a failed assassination? What was their plan? If I died, I'd never fulfill my mother's dying wish. I had to stay alive. Even if I survived the Fae forest of Gwerhune and all of its dangerous creatures, the moment I entered that castle, I'd be living my last moments.

"A thousand condolences, my king." I bowed again. When men were grieving, they often struck out at the nearest person.

Master padded closer and lifted my chin with his thick thumb. "Enough groveling. Listen."

"Aye, Master."

"When my retinue found her and her guards..." The king's gravelly voice trailed off and he coughed.

I'd seen the crown princess while on a job at Earl Finton's estate. She had been dancing with cousins, her light brown skin and long black hair so similar to the late queen's.

When the king turned at the base of the three steps that led away from this greeting section of the chamber and into the bedroom quarters, the sun showed his eyes and his unshed tears. His cheeks drew in tightly, shifting his beard so that it brushed his gold-hemmed cloak and the bronze clasp at his throat. "My men found... Near her body, they found a sigil ring."

My ears perked up. I hadn't heard about this. I was aware that she had been killed with a blade to the throat and that the killer had burned her body, perhaps in some attempt at a magic ritual.

The king removed a circle of pale gold from the plum and black leather pouch at his belt. He held up the sigil ring and Master hurried over to look closely.

"A hare and a fern..." Master squinted. He was losing his sight in his old age. "What else is on the ring, my king?" he asked, his voice more humble than I'd ever heard it. He sounded like a stranger instead of the man who had raised me.

"There is also a mace and a drumstone."

Master let out a small gasp.

"Yes, this is the sigil ring of the Fae king." The king's lips twisted into a grimace. He was holding back tears. My heart pinched and I wanted to say something. But what? I had no comforting role to play here or anywhere. Clearing his throat, the king continued, "He had his assassins kill our kingdom's most treasured daughter and he left his ring here as a warning."

Master motioned to a one-eyed servant named Rori, who had once helped me sneak back into Isernwyrd after a night out drinking with Raulian.

Master mouthed the words *Bring wine* to Rori before facing the king again.

"What do you believe this horrifying act warned us of?" Master asked.

The king rubbed a hand through his hair and exhaled roughly. "To remain on our side of the Veil. They will continue to trade with us because it benefits them, but the Fae king wants us to remember our place beneath his boot. He has flat-out refused my attempts to draw up a proper treaty to protect resources on both sides of the Veil. Fae are haughty creatures. Deceitful animals. All they care to trade away is their Fae gold."

The way he spat gold made it seem like it was worthless. The gold had worked just fine to buy King Darrew the lumber, sails, and men to build a new fleet of ships designed by the Deigs people. He was currently using said fleet to attack the western kingdoms beyond the White Sea.

Regardless of the strange way the king denied his need and past use of Fae gold, he certainly had a good reason for hating the Fae king, the Ruler of the Realm of Lights. His own daughter had been slain by our new neighbors. Not that the Seelie Fae were actually new to the world; they had been behind the

Veil and had recently thinned it enough to engage in trade.

"I will have revenge." Lifting his fist, the king squeezed his fingers until his knuckles were white. "We all will." He whirled on me, his grief giving way to rage. "You will kill him in the most painful way possible."

The image of a four-pronged leaf flashed through my mind. "With cherubium root." It was the worst way to die. Painful. Slow. And the victim couldn't cry out for help or thrash about. No antidotes either. It didn't matter though. I was not going. Not a chance. I would escape Master's network and get away from him for good. Maybe Raulian would come with me.

But only if we could cut out our curse runes.

Everyone who had tried that—two that I knew of personally—had died from self-inflicted wounds or by Master's stick. But I wasn't just anyone... A memory of Oolard's broken legs and his corpse left to rot in the wasteland blinked across my mind's eye.

Sick glee poured across the king's features and more tears glistened in his gaze. "Cherubium root. Yes." He turned to Master. "She is the best choice. I can tell by the look of her."

He had no idea I was plotting escape rather than his impossible task.

Get The Fae King's Assassin today!
Available in ebook, print, or audiobook.

And don't forget to get Kingdom of Spirits, Bound by Dragons Book Two!

Acknowledgments

It always takes a village to write a book and I'm so grateful for mine!

Thanks to my Dragon Divas—Rachel, Ali, Megan, Sarah, Kelly, and Erin—your cheering and ideas make my stories so much more epic.

Thank you to my Facebook group, Alisha's Dragon Den, for the support and love you've given me and my characters since the beginning!

Thank you to my local author pals, the Taco Crew, for giving me brainstorming help and all the queso. Sarah, Lauren, Erica, Kristin, and Myra, I adore you forever.

Huge thanks to those who have read any/all of my books and have reviewed, spread the word, or emailed me to gush about our imaginary friends. Dear Readers, I couldn' t do this amazing job without you!

Last but not least, thank you to my family for putting up with me being spacey when plotting and dragging you to every fantasy related events within a 100 mile radius.

ABOUT THE AUTHOR

Alisha Klapheke is a USA Today bestselling author of fantasy. When she isn't penning crazy novels about dragons, elves, and Fae, she travels the world in search of unique inspiration. She also teaches MMA (mixed martial arts) with her husband, Daniel, at their dojo just south of Nashville. Alisha has two amazing kids, a couple of ridiculous cats, and a creek in front of her house like she always dreamed about.

Feel free to follow on Instagram or join her fan group, Alisha's Dragon Den, on Facebook.

Also by Alisha Klapheke

Kingdom of Spirits

The Fae King's Assassin

Dragons Rising

And many more...

Go to alishaklapheke.com for a full list of books and where to start.

Thanks for reading!